DATE DUE

APR 25 '94			
JAN 3 95			Alkali County

DEMCO 38-29.

Maverick Books, Inc.
Box 549
Perryton, Texas 79070
(806) 435-7611

Alkali County Tales

or

If at First You Don't Succeed, Get a Bigger Hammer

by John R. Erickson

Illustrations by Gerald L. Holmes

Distributed to the Trade by:
Texas Monthly Press, Inc.
P. O. Box 1569
Austin, Texas 78767-1569
(512) 476-7085

First printing, First Edition 1984
Second printing, September 1986
Third printing, April 1987

Manufactured in the United States of America

Maverick Books, Inc.
Box 549
Perryton, Texas 79070
(806) 435-7611

This one is dedicated to
my brothers and sisters:
Ellen and Don,
Scot and Lawren,
and Charles

Contents

The Spearmint Station

The other day, after the livestock sale was over, I drove out to the Alkali County Experiment Station. I pay a visit to the station at least once a month, and always for the same two reasons: first, to ask the resident scientist, Dr. Barley McOatwheat, if he will return the shovel he borrowed from me five years ago; and second, to observe a great mind at work.

Actually, the first reason is phony. I don't suppose McOatwheat will ever find the shovel, and I would be disappointed if he did, because then I would lose my excuse for going out to the dreary little cinderblock building east of town, which most folks around here call the "Spearmint Station." A guy needs a pretty good excuse for going there because for the past 20 years Dr. McOatwheat's research into the mysteries of science has managed to turn up absolutely nothing that relates to anything.

He came to Alkali County in 1955 with USDA's Grasshopper and Jackrabbit Survey. The project was poorly funded,

1

so the government furnished the block and mortar and McOatwheat had to build the Spearmint Station himself. It grew into a masterpiece of ineptitude, perhaps the only building in the United States that is neither plumb nor square, and that does not contain a single right angle or straight line. Light bulbs dangle from the ceiling on frayed cords. A mysterious network of exposed pipes meanders through the building; they are mysterious because Dr. McOatwheat does not yet have running water.

There is another mystery associated with the Spearmint Station. Nobody seems to know why it's still here. The Grasshopper and Jackrabbit Survey was completed in 1957, but McOatwheat continues to send his monthly reports to Washington, and Washington continues to send him enough money to keep the station open. Willie Onthenextranch may have come up with the answer. He says that Dr. McOatwheat is living in exile and just doesn't know it yet.

As usual, I slipped into the station as quietly as a thief and seated myself in the chair in the broom closet. Why is there a chair in the broom closet? I've wondered that myself. For five years there has been a chair in the broom closet, but not a single broom. I always hide in the closet, peek through a hole in the cinderblock wall and watch the great mind at work.

On this particular afternoon Dr. McOatwheat was dictating a report to his faithful secretary, Miss Mattie Sparrow. An old maid, Miss Mattie has devoted her life to Dr. McOatwheat and his work at the station. She believes it is only a matter of time until the world recognizes what she has known all along—that he is a genius. In her eyes, he can do no wrong. He is a brilliant man living among knot-headed farmers and ranchers who are simply not equipped to understand true genius.

In addition to her secretarial duties, Miss Mattie acts as McOatwheat's public defender against gossip. Among other things, it is rumored that he carries a pint of spirits in his coat

2

pocket. The scientist has assured Miss Mattie that this is false, and therefore it is. Woe unto the man who wonders aloud what causes that bulge in his pocket. "It is a hand warmer, sir," she will reply, drawing herself up like a mother lion. "Dr.

G.L. Holmes

McOatwheat suffers from poor circulation. He told me so himself."

Anyway. Dr. McOatwheat was dictating a report to Miss Mattie when I slipped in. He wore his usual black suit, wrinkled white shirt and wilted bow tie. His spectacles were pulled down on his nose and his socks did not match.

"All right, Mattie," he said, "we must get the results of this experiment down on paper before I forget it. I can't remember things the way I used to."

Sitting with her sharpened pencil poised over a stenographic pad, Miss Mattie looked up at the scientist with adoring eyes and said, "It's only human to forget, Doctor."

"Um, quite so," he muttered. Then, pulling on his chin and pressing his lips tightly together, he began. "Our question is this: once and for all, why does a chicken cross the road?" Miss Mattie sprang to her shorthand while Dr. McOatwheat paced the room. "This phenomenon has puzzled scientists for decades, and we still have not found the answer.

"In the late '50s the best research on the subject centered around the seasonal instincts of the chicken. It was widely accepted that, at certain times of the month, possibly related to the phase of the moon . . . "

McOatwheat stumbled over a chair and fell to the floor. In a matter of seconds, Miss Mattie was at his side, helping him to his feet. "Who put that idiot chair in the middle of the room?" he snarled.

"I did it, Doctor. It's all my fault."

The scientist grunted. "We must be more careful, Mattie. Now, where was I?"

Miss Mattie studied her notes. "Phase of the moon."

He scowled. "What was I talking about?"

"Chicken crossing road."

He rolled his eyes. "Um, I wonder what the moon has to do with chickens. Oh well, let's get on with it. My research on the behavior of chickens, based on 20 years of careful observa-

4

tion at this station, has convinced me that chickens do not—underline that, Mattie—do not cross the road merely to get to the other side. I believe that a chicken is not smart enough to know one side from another, but to substantiate this," he waved a bony finger over his head, "I must have staff and equipment and adequate funding! Get that down, Mattie, while I check some figures."

He left the room, darted into the broom closet, and was already swigging on the hand warmer before he saw me. I think he was surprised.

"Afternoon, Doc," I said. "I was just looking for my shovel."

The hand warmer disappeared as if by magic. The scientist drew his face into a thoughtful scowl. "Fine, thank you. I was just looking for some data, I wonder where Mattie put, it doesn't seem to be . . . "

I grinned and poked him in the ribs. "Doc, you weren't taking a little snort, were you?"

He looked me straight in the eyes. "I hope Mattie doesn't hear you, sir. She would wring your neck. Now, if you'll excuse me, I have an important report to get out." He strolled back into the office where Miss Mattie was waiting, her gaze filled with adoration. "I found those figures, Mattie. In order to continue this project on chickens, we must have funding of not less than $200,000. Does that sound reasonable?"

Miss Mattie sighed and clasped her hands together. "Dr. McOatwheat, if you have a fault, it's that you constantly underestimate your own worth."

He pulled on his chin for a moment. "You could be right, Mattie. Make that $500,000.

Willie Onthenextranch

It was just the kind of mess Willie Onthenextranch always seems to get himself into. You'd think a man living on a ranch in the Panhandle could ignore the 20th century and get away with it, but not old Willie.

It began when he got a questionnaire from the U.S. Department of Agriculture. It asked a lot of important questions, such as how many Chicanos/Native Americans/Blacks/Women did he have on his labor force? And did they hold responsible positions? And how many cubic meters of manure did his cows/horses/sheep/goats/chickens/ducks produce in an average year?

Willie, being a good citizen, spent an hour answering the questions. He wrote, "We raise camels on this ranch. We plant them in the fall, harvest them in July and grind them up to make Camel cigarettes. All my camels are broke to a flush toilet. All the toilets are equipped with manure meters. According to my records, each camel produced 35 filibusters of

6

manure last year. My wife, who is a woman, works with me on the ranch and holds the position of executive vice president, which is very responsible. Her wages are the same as mine. We're both trying to pay it off at the bank. The rest is none of your derned business.''

Willie was proud of this letter and showed it to me one day when I stopped in for coffee. ''Willie,'' I said after reading it, ''you're asking for trouble. They're not going to think this is very funny. It says here you can be prosecuted for giving false information.''

G. L. Holmes

"Then let 'em prosecute," he snarled. "If them beero-crats want to co-sign my note at the bank, I'll tell them every-thing they want to know. If all they want is free information, then they'll get just about what they pay for."

I shook my head. "I think that's a poor attitude. Listen, the Department of Agriculture is *our* department; they're on our side. They send out these questionnaires for a good reason."

"What's the good reason?"

There was a long silence. "Willie, just because you and I can't think of a `good reason doesn't mean there isn't one. There's always a reason for everything, and if I was you, I'd fill it out right."

He snatched the coffee cup out of my hand and poured the coffee back into the pot. "Well, you're partly right. There's reasons for some things. The reason you don't get any more of my coffee is that it's too expensive to waste on a fool. And the reason you're leaving my house right now is that you've got nuthin' to say that I want to hear." He opened the screen door and pointed the way to my pickup. "Bye bye."

"Gee, you get awful snuffy."

"And so's your old man."

Well, he mailed out the questionnaire and two weeks later he was notified by USDA than an investigating team was on its way to his ranch. The department had found some irregularities in his questionnaire, and they were sending a team of experts out from Washington to gather some more information.

Willie told me later that he was worried when they drove up. By then, he didn't think his little joke was so funny. The USDA had sent a team all the way from Washington to look at his camels, and he was going to be hard put to show them any.

The team was headed by a young woman named Ms. Pesker, whose title was first deputy assistant to the under-secretary of the bureau of agri-morals, in the non-productive division of the U.S. Department of Agriculture. With her on the team of experts were two attorneys and an accountant.

They got right down to business. Ms. Pesker said they wanted to see his camels. Willie swallowed hard and drove them out into the pasture. He showed them his herd of Angus cows.

"Well, there they are," he said. The experts studied the cows from every angle, while Willie held his breath and wondered how he would adjust to prison life.

Ms. Pesker sensed something was wrong. "I thought camels were brown."

"Eh . . . you're thinking of Arabian camels, ma'am. Arabian camels are brown, but these are hybrid camels. Hybrids are almost always black."

"I see," she nodded, and all four experts began taking notes.

But one of the lawyers was not satisfied. "I was under the impression that camels were characterized by a type of hump or dual protuberance along the spine. I don't see anything like that on these creatures."

"Well, of course not," Willie explained. "We've bred the hump out of these camels. With the hump, it took the warbles too long to get out."

"You mean birds?"

Willie stared at him. "Huh?"

The lawyer smiled. "I say, do you mean birds? You mentioned warblers."

"Oh . . . yes," said Willie, "so I did. Warblers."

The lawyer was still puzzled. "I don't quite see the connection. What do birds have to do with camels, and why would that affect your breeding program?"

At this point Ms. Pesker intervened. "He breeds the hump out of his camels because it takes too long for the warblers to get out. Just write it down, Emory, you don't have to understand everything you hear." Emory began writing. "Well, everything seems to be in order here. Now we come to the serious part of the investigation: your wife."

"My wife?"

All at once Ms. Pesker's eyes flashed. "Why yes. Could it be that you don't believe women should be taken seriously? I remind you that sexual discrimination is against the law."

Willie said he wasn't trying to discriminate and wanted to know what the problem was with his wife. "You didn't indicate on your questionnaire whether she was Black, Chicano or Native American."

"I see. Well, her story is she's a white woman."

Ms. Pesker shook her head. "I'm sorry, that's not one of the categories. She's got to be either Black, Chicano or Native American."

Willie tried to argue but it didn't do any good. Finally, since his wife's great-great-grandmother had been one-eighth Cherokee, he told them she was a Native American. That seemed to please them, and Ms. Pesker announced that the investigation was over and they were ready to fly back to Washington.

As they were getting into their rented Chrysler, Willie asked. "Ma'am, how did you happen to get a job in the Department of Agriculture? What I mean is, where did you get your training in livestock?"

"Well, I've read lots of books," she replied, "but I got most of my training as a student leader in the beef boycott."

"I see," Willie nodded. "Well, do ya'll folks in the USDA have any advice for all the farmers and ranchers out here who are going broke?"

"Yes we do," she said. "If, in the process of going broke, you discriminate against Blacks, Chicanos, Native Americans or Women, we won't hesitate to file suit against you."

Willie tried to smile. "Boy, it sure is good to know that *our* department of government hasn't forgotten about us."

Ms. Pesker started the car. "No, we certainly haven't forgotten you. Now that we have your questionnaire on file, we'll be investigating you every six months."

As the car drove out of sight, Willie muttered, "If I ain't here in six months, honey, you might find me at the welfare office."

Smut

Every now and then me and Willie Onthenextranch get into a serious discussion. For us, a serious discussion is anything that goes beyond the weather report and how the cows are doing. We try to avoid serious topics, but now and then they come up.

That's what happened about a month ago. It was Willie's fault this time. I was trying to tell him how the grass looked in the west pasture, but he barged in. Seems he and the wife had gone into Alkali the night before to see a movie. The name of it was "One Fell Out of the Cuckoo Clock," and they'd heard it was a Walt Disney picture about a family of birds.

Well, it wasn't a Walt Disney, and it wasn't even about birds or clocks, and Willie was on the prod about it. He goes on the prod about once every two weeks. It may have something to do with the moon, I don't know.

"That was the nastiest picture I ever saw," he fumed. "It was even nastier than the movie we saw last year, and I didn't figger they could make 'em any worse than that. All they did was cuss. I was flat embarrassed. If you ask me, that kind of movie is nothing in the world but fonography."

I hadn't seen the movie, but I nodded anyway. I knew he had a box of donuts on top of the refrigerator, and I didn't want him to get sore at me.

"I'll tell you what," he went on, "I'm tired of all this fonography. You don't dare go to a movie nowadays. You can't read a good book, you can't watch tv, you can't even find a decent magazine. For Pete's sake, you'd think the American people don't do anything but shack up and cuss! Doesn't anybody have to work for a living anymore?

I shook my head and kind of glanced up at the box of donuts. Willie takes hints about like a buffalo.

"Well, something's got to be done about this fonography," he went on. "It's got to be stopped before the whole country goes to ruin."

I never did get the donut.

About a week later, Willie called me up and said there was a new committee in Alkali, the Citizens Concerned About Smut. It was having its first meeting that night, and he wanted me to go with him. I told him I'd already made plans for the night—eat too much supper and fall asleep in the chair—but he said I had a duty to somebody or other, and that someone had to do something about something or other, and I figured if it was all that important, maybe I ought to go.

We met in a room at the schoolhouse, and I'd guess there were about 25 head of concerned citizens. Mrs. Seltzer was the chair. (We don't say chairman anymore when it's a woman.) She called the meeting to order. Then we wrote up a statement of purpose, a constitution and a set of by-laws, voted on a meeting date, membership dues and officers. By this time it was 9 o'clock. Self-government is a precious freedom, but also a lot of trouble.

Then Mrs. Seltzer asked if anyone would like to make an

opening statement about smut. An old farmer on the back row raised his hand and stood up.

"Madame speaker, friends, citizens, ladies and gentlemen. This smut problem has got completely out of hand. I worry about it all day, and I dream about it at night. If we don't do something to control the spread of smut, this wheat won't make 10 bushel to the acre."

Mrs. Seltzer explained that we weren't talking about that kind of smut, and the farmer apologized and went home. Then Willie got up and made his speech on fonography. It was a jim dandy. Old Willie worked himself up into a regular fit, and when he sat down the audience gave him a big cheer.

One man at the back said he thought Willie ought to be appointed chairman of a subcommittee to look into ways of cleaning up the nasty language in movies that came to town. He was elected by acclamation.

He stood up again and gave another speech on how this was an important job and the future of Alkali was at stake and he wouldn't rest until he could say that our kids were not down at the Bijou Theater watching trash and fonography. When he finally shut up, the folks gave him another big hand of applause.

Then a lady got up and said she thought we ought to appoint another subcommittee to clean up the language in the town itself. "If we're going to clean up the Bijou," she said, "we might as well clean up the drug store and the pool hall." Willie seconded the motion and it carried.

Then a preacher got up. He said that if we were going to clean up the Bijou and the town, it was only fair to clean up the country too. (Right here, me and Willie traded glances.) "It's been brought to my attention," the preacher said, "that some of our fine stockmen use vile and profane language around their cattle and horses, especially at roundups. I think we should appoint another subcommittee to look into these abuses."

That motion passed, but with two dissenting votes—me and Willie's. Come to find out, we were the only two cow chasers in the audience. The rest were respectable citizens.

Well, all at once the room got quiet. Then Mrs. Seltzer cleared her throat and looked at Willie. "Maybe you should explain the difference between foul language at the Bijou and foul language on your ranch."

Willie's face turned as red as a branding iron, and he stood up. "On my place you don't have to pay two dollars to hear someone cuss. It's free. It's always been free, and it'll continue to be free until the Commonists take over the country and tell us what to say. Now, I don't know how many Commonists we've got in this room, but the first snoopin' son-of-a-gun who comes out to my roundup . . . "

There's no need to go into all the details. Willie got impeached about half an hour after he was elected, and we walked out of the meeting. On the way home, Willie cussed the Citizens Concerned About Smut, member-by-member, and he was just finishing up on Mrs. Seltzer when we pulled up in front of my house.

"I don't know what's got into people these days," he sighed. "They just seem to lose their head."

"Yalp."

"They don't know the difference between good cussin' and bad cussin.' "

I agreed. "Well, I guess we could form a Cattlemen's Committee For The Preservation of Nasty Talk."

He glared at me. "Are you trying to be funny?"

I denied the charge and said good night.

Federal Inspection

It was your typical Indian summer afternoon: clear, warm and still. Out at the Alkali County Spearmint Station, the last fly of the season was buzzing around the office. When it flew too close to Miss Mattie Sparrow, she looked up from her sewing, gave it a menacing glare, and said, "Scat, you nasty thing!"

Instead of scatting, it landed on her desk. It was big, green and, as she had observed, nasty. She stared at the fly for a moment, wondering what she would do about it. Ordinarily, she would have called upon Dr. Barley McOatwheat to execute it and remove it from the building, while she looked the other way. But at the moment Dr. McOatwheat was in one of his dormant (sound asleep) periods, which often preceded his most brilliant scientific discoveries. She didn't want to disturb him.

She reached for the broom, which stood in the corner, raised it over her head, took careful aim, closed her eyes and turned her head, and Whap! Her aim was perfect, and death was instantaneous.

This broke the silence, and all at once Dr. McOatwheat exploded out of his chair. "That's it, Mattie! I've got it!" With the index finger of his right hand raised above his head, he stumbled toward her desk. "I've just solved one of the most vexing problems facing mankind in this century."

"Mercy!"

"This invention will change the course of history. The

future of the human race begins today, Mattie, right here in this laboratory. Prepare for dictation!"

Miss Mattie dropped her sewing, snatched up a pencil and pad, and sat poised at her desk, while McOatwheat clasped his hands behind his back and began pacing in front of her.

"It all came to me in a flash, in a blaze of inspiration. I don't wish to frighten you, Mattie, but what you write down in the next thirty minutes will determine the course of human events."

She gasped and placed one hand over her heart. "Oh my stars."

"Silence!" The scientist stopped pacing and placed the tips of his fingers against his temples. "Now let me reach into the vapors and bring back the revelation word for word."

At that moment, the front door opened and in walked a young woman wearing a yellow hat and carrying a clipboard in her hands. "Good afternoon, I am Ms. Picki with the United States Department of Safety, Health and Happiness. This installation is under federal inspection. Please remain seated and do not try to leave the building." She looked at her watch and wrote the time down on her pad. "I must warn you that any attempt to conceal evidence or to misrepresent the facts to a federal investigator can result in prosecution, fines, imprisonment, deportation and further investigation."

McOatwheat scowled. "Mattie, give the lady a dollar and send her on her way. We have important work to do."

A weak smile fluttered over Mattie's mouth. "But Doctor, I don't think that's what she wants."

"Good. Get her out of here. Now, where was I?" He closed his eyes and pressed his fingers against his temples again.

"Who is that man?" Ms. Picki demanded.

18

"Why, Dr. Barley McOatwheat, our resident scientist and one of America's most brilliant . . . "

"Why isn't he wearing a hard hat?"

"Well, I . . . really don't know. But do you suppose you could come back . . . "

"This is very serious." Ms. Picki made a note of it on her pad. "Very, very serious." She stalked over to McOatwheat, who had kept his back to her from the moment she had walked in the door. "Sir, this installation is funded by the Department of Agriculture, and I must ask . . . "

"Go away."

" . . . why you are not wearing a hard hat."

"Go away!"

"Agriculture involves animals which can cause serious injury to the head."

"Mattie, get her out of here!"

"Dr. McOatwheat," Ms. Picki persisted, "I suggest you find your hard hat and begin wearing it immediately."

McOatwheat plugged a finger into each of his ears and yelled, "Prepare for dictation, Mattie!"

Ms. Picki sighed. "Very well, I shall have to issue a citation." She began writing one out.

"Are you ready, Mattie? Here it comes. Subject: Generation of Electricity Using the McOatwheat Bovine-Mandible Technique."

Ms. Picki tore the citation off her pad and handed it to him. When she saw that his ears were plugged, she seized one of his arms and unstoppered the corresponding ear. "Dr. McOatwheat, I have issued a citation . . . "

"What's wrong with her?" he screamed to Mattie. "Is she crazy? Tell her I can't concentrate with all this noise!"

" . . . for non-compliance of federal safety regulations. It is a very serious offense."

When she tried to hand him the citation, he threw up his

hands, fled to the bathroom and slammed the door. Ms. Picki followed and rapped on the door.

"Dr. McOatwheat, I advise you to come out immediately."

"Don't leave your post, Mattie!" he shouted in the echoing bathroom. "We must get this down!"

Ms. Picki slipped the citation under the door. A moment later it reappeared, shredded into a dozen pieces. Shaking her head, she noted this on her pad and walked back to Mattie's desk. "Do you wear safety goggles when you type?" Mattie said no. "Safety gloves when you handle carbon paper?" No again. "When was the last time this office held a hurricane drill?"

"But we don't have hurricanes."

"I see," she nodded, as her pencil swooped down to the pad. "Therefore you feel you can violate the regulations on hurricane safety. I've noted that."

The bathroom door opened and McOatwheat stuck his head out. "Mattie, get this down: five-year-old cows, bubble-gum and generators!" He disappeared and the door slammed. Mattie wrote it down.

Ms. Picki examined Mattie's desk. "Who killed this fly?"

"Why . . . I did. He was . . . "

Did you have a permit?"

"A what?"

"I see." Down went the pencil. "Killing a fly without a permit. The remains will have to be buried in a licensed sanitary disposal area, otherwise you will be cited for further violations." Suddenly, Ms. Picki leaned down and looked Mattie straight in the eyes. "Do you feel you're being exploited?" Mattie shook her head. "Are you happy in this job?" Mattie nodded. "But are you really happy?" Mattie said she was. "But are you really really happy?"

Mattie was so flustered by this time, she burst into tears. "Yes, yes, yes, I am!"

Ms. Picki beamed a triumphant smile. "Then why are you crying? Of course you're not happy! You're miserable, you're exploited, you're working in an unhealthy and unsafe environment. But fear not, because I am closing down this installation today." She threw back her head and waited for Miss Mattie to cheer.

Mattie stared at her. The tears dried on her cheeks. She rose from her chair and fetched the broom from the corner. "I think it's time for you to leave."

Ms. Picki blinked. "But I've come to save you."

"Honey," Mattie took a practice swing, "I think you'd better save yourself while there's still time."

She began backing toward the door. "But I . . . hey, listen, I've got to warn you that I'm a black belt in karate."

Mattie advanced. "Well I'll swan, and I'm a black belt at busting heads with a broom."

Ms. Picki fled and jumped into her car. "I shall have to report this incident!"

"That will be fine, dearie, and if you ever come back here, I shall have to wring your little neck."

Ms. Picki zipped up the window and roared off. Mattie went back inside and found Dr. McOatwheat waiting. "Good work, Mattie! Very well said. Now, to your post!"

Mattie froze and sniffed the air "DOC-tor McOat-wheat, have you been drinking?"

The scientist rolled his eyes and covered his mouth with his hand. "Er, well, eh, um, I wouldn't put it that way . . . exactly."

Whap! "Ungrateful hound, you've been drinking behind my back!" Whap!

McOatwheat began circling the office, with Miss Mattie and her broom right behind him. "But Mattie, we must record

21

my discovery." Whap! "You see, I believe we can generate electricity by administering bubblegum to five-year-old cows . . . " Whap! " . . . and installing tiny generators on their jaw-bones." Whap! "As they chew, an endless stream of . . . " Whap! " . . . ouch, electricity will flow to our . . . " Whap! "Mattie, please, I was under a terrible strain. I didn't know what I was doing. Help!"

Whap!

Good Neighbors

I stopped in to see Willie Onthenextranch last week. It was hot and dry, a typical summer day in these parts. And I found Willie in his typical summer mood. As I walked toward the shade tree he was sitting under, I said, "Good morning, neighbor."

He glared at me from under his hat and replied, "Drop dead."

I wasn't offended or particularly surprised. Hot weather makes Willie about as jolly as a gila monster. It seems to bring out all the bad parts of his personality and make them worse. I've noticed that cold weather has the same effect on him. Usually in May and October he'll cheer up for a few days to the level of a rattlesnake.

I pulled up a chair and sat down, took off my straw hat and laid it on the grass. I saw that Willie had a big glass of iced tea. "I don't suppose you have another glass of that tea around do you?"

"Nope."

I waited for a minute. "I guess it would be too much trouble to make up some more."

"That's right."

He glared at me, just waiting for me to say something else. I just shrugged. A minute later, when he wasn't looking, I snared a big nasty grasshopper and dropped it into his tea glass. If I had to suffer the heat without iced tea, I wanted him to have an opportunity to suffer with me. I was studying the clouds when he found my gift.

"Dad-burned ding-busted pig-nosed grasshoppers!" he roared, pitching the tea out onto the grass. "Get out of there, you garden-destroying son of a codfish!"

I waited for him to settle down. "Speaking of gardens, how's yours doing this year, Willie?"

He narrowed his eyes and curled his lip. "What do you think? When the grasshoppers are eating ice cubes, how do you suppose the tomato vines are doing?"

I thought for a minute. "Real good?"

"Sure, they're doing great. I put out ten Porters and seven Juicy Wonders, and I ain't got a stalk left. The grasshoppers picked 'em as clean as a goose."

"How did your potatoes turn out?"

"Didn't dig a hill," he growled. "Didn't see a spud. Potato bugs ate the tops, coons dug up the rest."

"How about your turnips?"

"Horses ate 'em."

"Onions?"

"Too dry."

"Radishes?"

"Dead."

I could see it was time to change the subject. "How do the cattle look?"

"I've never seen cattle look so poor at this time of the year."

25

"But the market's pretty strong."

"It'll bust, you just wait. I'm predicting 20-cent calves by fall."

"Radio says we might get rain tonight."

"Oh, it'll rain all right—in Formosa and Brazil!"

That was about all of Willie's gloom I could stand, and I was still hacked about not getting any tea. I decided to straighten him out. "Willie, the trouble with you is that you have a lousy attitude."

He turned his head around and stared at me. "What?"

"I said you've got a lousy attitude. You'd find bad luck even if it was running away from you." He grunted at this. "And I'll tell you something else. A lot of people in Alkali County find you a little hard to take sometimes."

"Oh yeah?" He stood up and put his hands on his hips. "Anybody we know?"

"Yours truly, for one. Now and then I get tired of your gloomy moods."

"Well," he was getting a little snuffy by now, "we can sure remedy that little problem. Why don't you just load yourself into that pickup yonder and light a shuck?"

I sighed. "Well, I'm sorry you feel that way, Willie. It's been a long friendship."

"Awful long."

"And I was just getting to where I liked you a little bit."

"Never had that problem with you."

"And of course you're losing your best neighbor."

"Who still owes me five bales of bright alfalfa, which you can drop off the next time you're passing through, and I want them from the middle of the stack, and don't forget to bring back them posthole diggers either."

Now I stood up. "Well now, if you're going to dot the I's and cross the T's, let's just do some figgerin' here. I believe you've had my roofing hatchet since 1976, and there's that joint of two-inch pipe you snitched last winter."

26

"I didn't snitch it," he came right back, "because you borrowed it from me in 1970 when you were too lazy and sorry and worthless to go to town and buy one."

"Now just hold on there," I said. "I took that joint of pipe as payment for two fan sections you borrowed back in 1967 because you were too tight to keep your own windmills running."

Willie hitched up his pants. "Them two fan sections, mister, was partial payment for the door *your* sorry old bull tore out of *my* stock trailer in 1964."

"If my bull was sorry," I yelled, "it was because he'd spent the winter in your pasture, and the way you operate a ranch, a cow brute's lucky to make it till green grass!"

Willie nodded his head. "Yeah, and I never did get pasture bill for that either."

"Because I wintered half your heifer crop that year, that's why, and if anybody had pasture bill coming, it was me!"

"I can't keep my heifers at home if you don't keep up your dad-danged fences!"

"You're the one who put in those three rotten wires and toothpick posts!"

"That's because the survey was wrong and you've got one foot of my grass on your side of the fence, and one of these days we're going to replace the whole son-of-a-gun and I'm going to get my grass back where it belongs!"

"That suits me!" I yelled. "I'm tired of hearing you complain about it. Let's start on it right now."

"Fine!" Willie hollered back. "And then we won't have to speak for the rest of our lives!"

We marched right down to the barn and started dragging out the diggers, the stretchers, rolls of wire, posts, hammers, and all the rest of the junk. It was powerful hot, and before long sweat was dripping off the end of Willie's nose. After a bit, he stopped and wiped his forehead on his shirt sleeve.

"Awful danged hot, ain't it?"

27

He was waiting for me to say calf-rope, but I wasn't going to. "It's just right for building fence."

We loaded some more stuff, and the sweat poured. Willie sighed. "Listen, if we've got to have a falling out, why don't we wait for cooler weather?"

"Nothing doing. I want our accounts settled today. I don't care how hot it is."

"Well, at least we could stop for a glass of tea, couldn't we?"

I straightened up. "Tea! Why you old bucket of guts, if you'd offered me a glass of tea an hour ago, we wouldn't be here right now!"

He raised his brows and grumbled something under his breath. "Huh. One little glass of tea. Well, how was I supposed to know you were so danged sensitive?"

"Willie, the trouble with you . . . "

"I know, I know," he growled. "Let's quit this fuss and have some tea."

We headed for the house.

"Willie, the trouble with you is that you're just too sweet and kind and generous."

"Yalp."

"And open-hearted and cheerful."

"Uh huh, that's what everybody says."

Half an hour later, after we'd each had two big glasses of iced tea, Willie gave me one of the nicest compliments he's ever handed out. "You know," he said, "having neighbors is a pain in the neck, but I believe having enemies could be even worse."

Pranks

Someone once said that the human race can be divided up into two categories. Into the first category you put the ones who don't fit into the second, and into the second you put the ones who don't fit into the first. That sounds good on paper, but I never found much use for it myself.

If it was me, I'd say the human race could be divided up into those who play practical jokes and those who get jokes played on them. You'd have to put Willie Onthenextranch into the joker category, and Dr. Barley McOatwheat in with those poor souls who go through life never suspecting that there are people in the world who lie awake at night thinking of pranks to play on them.

If there was ever a man who was born to be the butt of a joke, it was our favorite scientist, Dr. McOatwheat. Here is a man who is so brilliant, whose mind operates on such a high intellectual level, whose thoughts are so advanced that it puts the rest of us to shame. Of course he has a little trouble with the simple things in life, such as finding the bathroom, starting his car, eating a sandwich, remembering which pocket he put his wallet in and then locating that pocket.

You could put a can of pork and beans in front of McOatwheat, and if Mattie Sparrow wasn't around to show him how to work the can opener, he'd starve to death. If it hadn't been for Miss Mattie's looking after him, McOatwheat would have gone to the bone yard long ago.

Now, on the other side we have Willie Onthenextranch —rancher, crackpot and practical joker. Willie is drawn to McOatwheat just as an ant is drawn to a picnic. He can't resist stopping in at the Spearmint Station and playing some prank on McOatwheat. And the funny part is that McOatwheat never catches on. It doesn't matter how often Willie stops in or how many pranks he pulls, McOatwheat always falls for the next one.

It's a different story with Miss Mattie. She can recognize a shark when she sees one, and over the years she's done her best to protect her sainted doctor from the "mindless rabble," which is her favorite word for Willie. And for me too, I guess. But Miss Mattie can only do so much.

Willie's jokes aren't particularly original, but that doesn't seem to matter. I don't know how many times he's jacked up McOatwheat's Hudson Hornet and put the back end on cinder blocks. McOatwheat's response never varies. He guns the motor for three or four minutes, gets out, opens the hood, stares at the machinery (which he doesn't understand and won't touch), throws up his hands, walks home and calls a wrecker.

The owner of the wrecker service caught on after the second time. Now he goes out and removes the cinder blocks and sends the bill to Willie Onthenextranch. But McOatwheat hasn't caught on to it yet.

And then there was the time Willie ran a wire from a spark plug to the driver's seat, leaving a bare end exposed in the place usually occupied by the scientist's posterior. McOatwheat figured out that the faster the motor ran, the more shock he got, so for the next two weeks he drove everywhere in first gear. Finally, he took it to a mechanic.

Another of Willie's favorite jokes is to hijack McOatwheat's favorite pipe, which he often smokes while he is performing scientific experiments, and to load it with gunpowder. I had the good fortune of being present once when McOatwheat lit up.

It was a spectacle I shall never forget. For a moment the doctor's head disappeared in a cloud of fire, sparks and smoke. Then from inside the cloud we heard a voice say, ''Beware of these matches, Mattie, they're explosive!'' I had to carry Willie to the pickup after that, he was laughing so hard, and the next day he had to start wearing his truss again.

Then there was his latest prank, which he pulled this summer. It was a hot day and Willie had gone into Alkali to run an errand or two and then loaf. He was on his way to the pitch parlor when he saw McOatwheat's Hudson Hornet parked on Main Street. Well, that was just too much of a temptation for old Willie.

The fireworks stand was open at the south end of town, so he jumped into his pickup, streaked out there and bought two of those car bombs that whistle, explode and then make lots of smoke. He streaked back to town and installed both of them under the hood of McOatwheat's Hudson. Then he went into the pitch parlor and told all the loafers what was about to happen. Within minutes, a crowd was lurking in every doorway up and down Main Street, waiting to see the show.

The excitement started when McOatwheat didn't come out of the drug store, didn't get into the car and didn't start the motor—but Miss Mattie Sparrow did. She must have borrowed his car to run an errand. She came out of the drug store, went straight to the Hudson in that prissy little walk of hers, climbed in, started the motor and pulled out of the parking place. The bombs went off when she was right in the middle of

31

Main Street. She hit her brakes when the whistling started. Then ka-blooey! ka-blooey!

Smoke poured out of every crack and from under the car. Miss Mattie squealed like a panther. I guess she thought she was about to be roasted alive. Then, instead of just opening the door and stepping out, she bailed out the window. When she did, 90 per cent of the loafers in Alkali County got their first glimpse of Miss Sparrow's petticoats.

Well, things got out of hand. Miss Mattie fainted in the middle of the street, traffic came to a halt and merchants who were not in on the joke rushed out to fight the blaze. Within minutes, the fire department, the police department and the ambulance were rushing to the scene with their sirens blaring, and Willie Onthenextranch was roaring out of town as fast as his pickup would run.

Nothing stinks quite as badly as a practical joke that has gone sour. The town officials were outraged. The chief of police was quoted in the newspaper as saying that he wouldn't sleep until he had captured the heartless fiend who was behind this dastardly act of mischief.

That, of course, was a slight exaggeration. Our chief of police can be found almost any Sunday morning sleeping in his pew at the Baptist church, and I have every confidence that in the case of Miss Mattie's bomb, his love of sleep triumphed over his inflamed conscience.

The story was big news for a week or two, then it died down. Though there were a number of witnesses to the explosion, none of them seemed to know who the culprit might have been. One fellow reported that he had seen a band of Arab terrorists in town that very morning, but this did not check out. Within a few weeks, the whole matter was forgotten, and most of Alkali County went back to sleep for the summer.

Well, almost forgotten. There was one small incident which occurred two days after the bombing. It was not reported in the newspaper and very few people ever heard about it.

It seems that Willie Onthenextranch was in Alkali (looking very innocent, I'm sure) and his pickup was parallel parked in front of the pitch parlor. When he had finished his business in town, he jumped into the pickup and, as is his custom, went roaring off.

Only this time he left his back bumper sitting beside the curb. Apparently the log chain had fallen out of the back of his pickup. One end had tied itself around the trailer hitch while the other had attached itself to a utility pole.

Willie refused to believe there was any connection between this freak accident and the case of Miss Mattie's bomb. As he pointed out, Miss Mattie was a sweet old dumpling who was simply not capable of seeking revenge. However, he did confide to me that the next time he saw Miss Mattie, she smiled at him for the first time in 27 years.

Fishing

It was getting toward the end of summer. Fall was in the air, but it was still hotter than blazes. I had been around checking the water in all the stock tanks, and on my way home I stopped in to see Willie Onthenextranch.

His pickup was parked in front of the barn and he was underneath doing some work. I walked up and said, "Well, Willie, is it warm enough for you today?" He didn't answer, so I said, "What's the matter, can't you find the dipstick?" Still no answer. "Willie, did you crawl under there to take a nap?" He still didn't answer, and that worried me. You hear all the time about people dropping dead with strokes and heart attacks.

I got down on my hands and knees and looked under the pickup. What I saw made my hair stand on end. The top half of Willie's body was gone! There wasn't anything under there but a pair of legs. Speaking of heart attacks, I almost had one myself.

Just then he came walking out of the barn. "You're awful danged snoopy, aren't you. What do you want?"

34

What I'd seen under the pickup was a pair of jeans stuffed with gunny sacks, and with a pair of boots stuck into the legs. A dummy, in other words, which made two of us.

"Willie, you old reprobate, what do you mean putting a dummy under your pickup?"

He glared at me. "It's my ranch, ain't it? I guess I can put anything I want under my pickup."

I took a deep breath. "Well, you gave me a terrible scare. I thought you'd been amputated at the waist."

"How was I supposed to know you'd come up and snoop around?" he snarled. "Most folks drive past and think, 'There's old Willie, hard at work in the heat of the day.' Which is what they're supposed to think."

I nodded. "So you were in the barn loafing and just didn't want anyone to know about it."

"I wouldn't call it loafing."

"And what would you call it?"

He rubbed the stubble on his cheek. "I was planning a fishing trip, if you just have to know."

"A fishing trip!"

He scowled. "Yeah, a fishing trip. What's so criminal about that? Everybody else in the United States takes off and goes fishing, why can't I? Is there something in the Constitution that says a rancher can't take a little vacation now and then?"

"Well . . . "

"Listen, I'm so sick of this ranch I could spit. Hot and dry, hot and dry, hot and dry! This country ain't fit for a stray dog. I'm tired. I'm fed up. I'm going fishing, and if you don't like it, you can march right over to that tree yonder and hang yourself, and I'll furnish the rope."

"Well now . . . "

"Or you can go with me."

"Hm, well . . . "

"Good!" He clapped his hands together. "I've got it all

figgered. We'll leave right now and drive over to a spot on the Gypsum River. They tell me there's catfish in there as big as a man, and all you have to do is say 'beef liver' over the water and they'll jump onto your stringer. We'll camp out for three days, and we won't even think about cattle, fences or windmills. Let's go."

"Now hold on, Willie." He'd already started for the barn. "We'd better make some plans and get some gear together."

"Will you quit yappin'? I've been working up this trip for two weeks. I've got everything figgered and packed and ready to go."

"Did you remember . . . "

He showed me the palm of his hand. "I remembered everything. Get your toothbrush and let's go."

An hour later we were on our way, with Willie's pickup loaded down with enough junk to keep an army supplied for a month. If he'd forgotten anything, I couldn't imagine what it was.

We drove for two hours over rough roads and feed trails, and finally we came to his spot on the river. As soon as the pickup bounced to a stop, he was out the door. He grabbed his rod and ran to the water.

"Come on!" he yelled over his shoulder. "Them giant catfish are just waiting for us to pull 'em out!"

"Don't you want to unload the stuff?" I asked.

"Later, after we catch our supper."

"Uh, Willie . . . you didn't bring any food?"

"The river's full of food. Come on."

So I grabbed my pole and ran down to the river. When I got there Willie was so excited his hands were shaking. In his excitement, he got his line tied up in a knot as big as your fist. I thought he would go nuts. He raved and cursed and finally cut the knot out with a pocket knife and rigged up another hook.

"Where did you put the beef liver?" I asked. His eyes darted from side to side. "Willie, did you forget the bait?"

"Anybody knows that grasshoppers make the best catfish bait anyhow." And off he went into the brush, chasing grasshoppers like a lunatic.

Finally we got baited up and put our lines in the water. Willie got the first strike. His cork went under and his pole bent down. "Ha ha!" he cried. "What did I tell you?" He went on to land a magnificent five pound mud turtle. I cannot reveal what he said to the turtle.

We fished until dark and didn't get another nibble. I suggested that we stop and set up camp. Willie agreed. He was dejected but not defeated. "Catfish don't start biting until dark anyway."

Stumbling over willows and tamaracks and sunflowers we moved half a ton of camping gear down to the river bank. The tent alone must have weighed 200 pounds and was probably big enough to accommodate an outdoor revival meeting. But that was mere speculation. Since Willie forgot to bring a flashlight, we weren't able to set it up.

We built a campfire on the river bank and went back to fishing. It was then that the mosquitoes started moving in, clouds of them, and they all must have been as hungry as I was. "Willie," I said, "I think I already know the answer, but did you bring any mosquito dope?"

"The only dope I brought keeps talkin' and scarin' the fish away."

We fished in silence for the next two hours. We caught nothing. At midnight I reeled in my line. Willie did the same. As we crawled into our blankets, I pointed to a line of thunderstorms off to the west and wondered if, in addition to our other miseries, we would get rained on. Willie answered with a loud snore.

It must have been around 4 a.m. that I noticed the water

37

running through my blankets. At first I thought I had wet the bed. Then I heard a roaring sound, and in the moonlight I saw that we were now camped in the middle of a river swollen with a head rise. I leaped to my feet. The water was shin-deep and rising fast. I yelled at Willie and told him to run for his life.

By the time he woke up, the water was knee-deep and our camp had disappeared. Willie's circus tent was on its way to Fort Smith, and I'll bet it took out every water gap along the way.

We escaped with our lives and little else. We drove home in our drawers and T-shirts and prayed that Willie's pickup wouldn't break down on the way. Willie kept muttering, "I don't think my wife is going to believe this story."

We arrived at Willie's place in time to watch the sun rise over the sandhills. As I was about to drive off, he said, "Go ahead and say it. I know you've got some smart remark to make."

"Not at all, Willie. It was a wonderful vacation. I don't know when I've had so much fun. Catching grasshoppers and getting half-drowned was only part of the fun. The best part was sharing your charming personality, your sparkling wit, your . . . "

"Drop dead," he grumbled, and trudged off to the house.

His wife met him at the porch, glanced at his bare, pipecleaner legs, and gave him a look of utter astonishment. I stuck my head out the window and yelled, "Willie, whatever you do, don't tell her about the whisky and the wimmen!" And I drove off in a cloud of dust.

That was my little way of thanking him for the lousiest fishing trip I ever took.

Hunters

Most generally when you see a ranch advertised for sale, the ad starts off something like this: "A sportsman's paradise! Plenty of dove, quail, turkey and deer." That gives you a pretty good idea who's buying the ranches these days, but that's not the point.

Willie Onthenextranch says that if he ever buys another ranch—and it will have to be in the next life since he can only afford to support one bad habit at a time—if he ever buys another ranch, the ad he's going to look for will read something like this: "A sportsman's hell. No trees, no live water, no pretty scenery. Plenty of dove, quail, deer and turkey have starved out and left. Absolutely no wildlife."

Willie isn't anti-nature or anti-wildlife, but you mention the word "sportsman" around him and you'll think he's taken the rabies.

You see, he was visited by some hunters last year, and the experience left a sour taste in his mouth.

40

He's never had much hunting on his place, just a few doves and quail up and down the draws, so he never had much trouble with hunters. Then around the first of December, he found a pile of quail feathers, four empty dog food cans, six beer cans, sandwich bags, napkins, candy wrappers, potato chip bags, and two cardboard boxes.

"It looked like the Children of Israel had come through on their way out of Egypt," he told me later, "and the Lord had sent down a quick stop grocery from heaven."

Well, Willie being Willie, he went right up the flue. If they had just shot the quail and gone on, he might have forgotten about it. But that pile of garbage, that was a declaration of war. He drove to town and bought two dozen signs. Before the sun went down that afternoon, he had No Hunting signs at every gate and cattleguard on the place.

And two days later, they had all been taken down, chopped up, and burned. Back to town he went, found a sign painter, and had a special set of signs made up on sheet metal. These didn't just say No Hunting. They said things like "Scram" and "Git," and "Leave My Birds Alone, You ———." He put these up with new bolts and nuts. It cost him 50 bucks, but he figured the hunters would get the message.

Two days later, all those nice new signs were so full of buckshot holes, you could have read a newspaper through them. Well, to say that Willie was mad would be a huge understatement. He couldn't quit now until he got revenge.

For the next week, he didn't turn a tap on the ranch. When the sun came up in the morning, he was staked out on a hill overlooking the draw, and he stayed there with a pair of field glasses until dark. He was going to find out who those hunters were, and then he was going to teach them a lesson they'd never forget.

Nobody showed up for three days, but then Willie's patience was rewarded. A pickup pulled into the pasture, stopped at the draw, and two hunters got out. Willie didn't recognize their faces, but he got the license number of the pickup.

He'd already made his plan. When he got back to the house, he loaded a few things into his pickup and streaked down the road to town. At the courthouse, he checked the records and found the address of the owner. He backed his pickup into the front yard and unloaded two weeks' collection of trash. Then he got out his shotgun and started blasting at sparrows in the trees.

When the lady of the house came out on the porch, leaves and feathers and sparrows were falling like snow. When she asked what he was doing, he replied. "Why ma'am, I didn't think y'all would mind if I had me a little picnic here. Your old man seems to think that's the way things are done."

It was a real stroke of genius, and if Willie hadn't copied down the license number wrong, he might have won a moral victory. But he got the wrong house. The lady was a widow woman who didn't even own a gun. She called the cops and told them there was a wild man in her front yard. Willie spent the night in the county clink, and they didn't let him go until he'd been examined by a psychiatrist. (The psychiatrist said he was normal, which kind of surprised me.)

When he finally got back to the ranch, he found more bird feathers and more garbage. The hunters were still slipping in. By this time, he was eating nails and pitchforks, he was so mad. He went back to his stake-out on the hill, but this time he didn't take field glasses. He took a shovel, and he planned to use it for something beside digging.

Two days later, a pickup came into the pasture and stopped at the draw. Willie couldn't see who was inside, but he didn't need to. He marched down to the pickup and took the valve stems out of all four tires, and then he went hunting with his shovel.

He flushed the first one out of a plum thicket. Creeping up behind the man, Willie yelled, "Banzai, you garbagedumpin' son-of-a bucks!'' and dove into the thicket, swinging his shovel. Taken somewhat by surprise, the hunter tore up a quarter-mile of grass trying to quit the country and get away from Willie and his shovel.

To make a long story short, the man wasn't a hunter. He was a biology teacher who had stopped on Willie's ranch to gather bird nests for a class exhibit. During the chase, he stepped into a badgerhole and broke his ankle. Willie hauled him to the hospital, apologized, and got sued for 5000 dollars.

Well by this time Willie was fed up. In just one month he'd lost almost as much money on quail as he had on his cattle, so he made the only sensible decision he could make under the circumstances: he poisoned the quail. (I told him he

should have poisoned his cattle while he was at it, but he didn't.)

Well, that fixed the hunters. They came back and never fired another shot. And three days later, Willie received a little note in the mail informing him that he was being sued by two sportsman's clubs and three environmental groups for destroying wildlife. They won, of course, and Willie had to restock his entire ranch with quail, at his own expense.

A man can only stay mad so long, and then he becomes what the writers call "philosophical," which means wore out. Willie accepted his defeat philosophically. He put up a new set of signs: "Hunters Welcome," and "Hunt Our Birds," and "Please Avoid Shooting Cows." He brought in picnic tables and trash barrels, and even installed a nice little yellow outhouse.

I couldn't understand it. That just didn't sound like the Willie I knew, so one day I asked him about it. We were sitting out on the front porch, and off to the north we could hear the shotguns booming away.

"Willie," I said, "why did you just give up?"

A little sparkle came to his eyes. "Wait till they eat them birds. Heh, heh."

"What do you mean by that?"

"Them quail were special ordered. Fried up real nice and brown, I bet they'd just melt your mouth."

I studied him for a minute. "Do you mean melt *in* your mouth?"

He grinned. "Like I say, they were special ordered. Heh, heh. Raised on nothing but red peppers and bat hockey, heh, heh. Melt your mouth."

Cheap Protein

Last spring, when cattle prices started going up, the mood of folks in Alkali County went up with it. For the first time in four years, the country people had a little money to spend in town.

Somehow this news must have gotten back to Washington, because the government started getting nervous about the high price of beef. I happened to be out at the Alkali County Spearmint Station one afternoon in August when Miss Mattie Sparrow brought in the mail. There was a letter for Dr. Barley McOatwheat from the Federal Bureau of Cheap Food. It was marked "urgent."

The subject of the urgent letter was the high price of beef, but we didn't find that out right away because McOatwheat didn't bother to open it right away. He was in the middle of a scientific experiment and didn't want to be disturbed.

The subject of the experiment was the yellowjacket wasp, which toward the end of summer becomes quite a nuisance in this part of the world. McOatwheat's interest in the yellowjacket had been whetted several weeks earlier when he had gone to change his underpants. Apparently a wasp had crawled into his drawers and taken up residence. When McOatwheat pulled them on, he received a painful sting on the dorsal sitting-downer.

At that moment, he had vowed to unleash the wrath of science on the yellowjacket wasp. He spent the next two weeks collecting specimens for study—which is to say that he sent Miss Mattie out into the field with a butterfly net and a mayonnaise jar with orders to capture and chloroform as many of the creatures as she could find. He explained that this task had fallen to Miss Mattie, not because he was afraid of wasps, but because she was looking pale and needed some sunshine.

The day I visited the Spearmint Station McOatwheat was bent over a microscope, observing a wasp. When Miss Mattie came in with the urgent letter from the Bureau of Cheap Food, McOatwheat told her to sit down and prepare for dictation.

"But Doctor," she said, "the letter is marked urgent. Maybe you should . . . "

This must have broken his concentration, because he flew into a rage. "Urgent!" he bellowed. "What could be more urgent than the pain and sorrow caused by this unutterable creature? The wasp has scourged mankind since the dawn of history, and you might recall, Mattie, that one of the great minds of science was scourged as recently as two weeks ago. I am still suffering from the poison . . . which reminds me. I haven't taken my antitoxin today."

He reached into his hip pocket and pulled out a medicine bottle. On the label, someone had written in large crude letters, "Wasp Antitoxin. Two swallows five times a day. Keep out of the reach of pets and children."

McOatwheat took two swallows and gasped. Miss Mattie watched with a sorrowful expression, then said to me,

46

"The poor dear has had to take that wretched medicine to counteract the poison. It must be terrible. I can hardly bear to watch him take it."

He returned the bottle to his pocket. "It's terrible, Mattie, and if you weren't standing right over me and forcing it upon me, I'd sooner take my chances with the poison."

"Now Doctor," she scolded, shaking her finger at him, "you said the allergy specialist told you to take it for another two months. We must be brave."

"You're quite right, Mattie. I suppose good health is worth the sacrifice. Now," his finger shot into the air, "prepare for dictation!" Mattie scrambled for her notebook, and McOatwheat bent over the microscope.

"I observe on the left end of the insect a small, sharp appendage. The Latin name for this appendage is *Damnable stingerus,* but henceforth we shall refer to it by its more common name, the stinger. The wasp inflicts pain by plunging his harpoon into human skin and injecting a deadly poison. It has been reported that in some extreme cases, the very mention of this poison can produce a violent reaction in one who has suffered a sting, and the victim can be saved only by the immediate introduction of wasp antitoxin into the body system."

At that moment, McOatwheat seized his throat with both hands, let out a horrible gasp, and collapsed on the table. Miss Mattie screamed and rushed to the fallen scientist. "It's the poison! He's suffered a reaction! Quick, the antitoxin!" She propped up his head and forced half the bottle down his gullet.

It saved him.

"You snatched me back from the grave," he wheezed, fanning his face with his hand. "God bless you, Mattie."

I expected a lightning bolt to come down from heaven and strike him dead, but it didn't. He continued with the dictation.

47

"It is my judgment that the danger of wasp stings can be eliminated through the invention of tiny rubber pants which would be fitted on every wasp in the land. As long as the sword is kept in a sheath, so to speak, it cannot draw blood.

"Now, Mattie, if you will write that up in the form of a proposal, I will submit it to the Bureau of Insects, and perhaps we can obtain a research grant of. . . let's try for five million. We can always come down."

Miss Mattie nodded and finished her dictation. Then she held up the urgent letter from the Bureau of Cheap Food and handed it to him. "Now you had better attend to this, Doctor."

Swaying back and forth on his stool and looking rather bleary eyed, McOatwheat tore open the letter and read it aloud.

"Attention all experiment stations: We have received unconfirmed reports that ranchers in certain parts of Texas, Oklahoma and New Mexico are beginning to make a profit. Any cattleman in your area who is not losing money should be reported to the bureau at once. Citations will be issued.

"Futhermore, this bureau, with its mandated purpose of protecting the consumers of this nation, instructs all stations to submit a report (original plus 23 copies) on the following subject: 'Inexpensive and Nutritious Protein Substitutes For Beef in the Diet of American Consumers.' This report should include a protein analysis and several recipes."

Dr. McOatwheat closed his eyes and went into a period of deep concentration. When he began to snore, Miss Mattie called him back from the vapors and asked if he was ready to dictate his reply.

"Yes, yes, quite ready," he mumbled, getting to his feet. He began to pace back and forth in front of her desk. "Take a letter. Mattie, and mark it urgent.

"Dear whomever and etcetera: In response to your query about cattlemen who have made money in the livestock business, it has been called to my attention that the last rancher who ran a profitable cattle operation in this region was named Goodnight. Between 1876 and 1884 he made money."

McOatwheat paused, and while Miss Mattie was catching up on her shorthand, made another pass at the medicine bottle. It brought a glow to his cheeks, and he continued with the dictation.

"Now, to the matter of cheap protein which would take the place of beef in the diets of consumers: I strongly recommend stray cats."

Miss Mattie's head came up. "Did you say. . ."

"Stray cats! Yes indeed. Now let's see, they want a protein analysis." He stroked his chin. "Put this down, Mattie. We have tested cat meat and found it to contain 57 units of protein per cubic megaphone, which of course is very good.

"And as for recipes, I suggest that the meat either be fried, baked, boiled, broiled, broasted, roasted, toasted or barbecued, with a pinch of garlic salt and three potatoes. That's good enough, Mattie. Type 23 copies and send it."

He weaved back to the table and peered into the microscope. "I think rubber pants will conquer these wasps."

Mattie was glaring at him. "Dr. McOatwheat, what was in that medicine bottle?"

"Huh?" He scowled and blinked his eyes. "Why, tox antiwaspum, of course."

Mattie stood up and placed her hands on her hips, an ominous sign. "Let me see that bottle." It was not a request. It was an order. McOatwheat handed it to her and began studying the water stains on the ceiling. I think he knew what was coming next.

Miss Mattie unscrewed the cap and passed the bottle under her nose several times. Her face turned blood red and her eyes bulged behind her glasses. "DOCtor McOATwheat! This is not medicine. This is whisky!"

McOatwheat's face registered shock. "Whisky? You can't be serious, Mattie."

49

At that moment, I couldn't contain myself any longer. I laughed. McOatwheat saw his opportunity to escape Miss Mattie's wrath and seized upon it at once.

"Sir," he turned to me, "I have been tricked by an unscrupulous physician. That is no cause for levity, and I'll thank you not to laugh at my misfortune."

Miss Mattie's glare went from McOatwheat to me. "Yes, the very idea!"

"And," McOatwheat continued, shaking a bony finger in my face, "if you are suggesting that I prescribed whisky for myself, well sir, I must warn you that Mattie will not stand for such calumny."

"I certainly will not!" said Miss Mattie, reaching for a broom and putting it over her shoulder like a baseball bat. "If you can't show more respect to one of the great men of science, then maybe you ought to go home."

"Yes ma'am," I said on my way out the door. She didn't need to tell me twice.

Outside, I slipped around to the west window and looked in. McOatwheat was patting his secretary on the shoulder and trying to console her.

"Don't let it bother you, Mattie. You did the right thing. We can't expect the common people to understand our work."

Miss Mattie nodded and sniffled and looked into the face of her sainted doctor. "Dr. McOatwheat, say you didn't put whisky in that bottle."

McOatwheat lifted his eyes toward heaven. "Mattie, I give you my solemn oath: you didn't put whisky in that bottle."

Weather

Back in the fall, everyone was saying we were going to have a hard winter. The almanac predicted lots of snow and cold weather, and the lady down the road who tells the weather by onion rings was calling for the same.

So nobody in the Panhandle was surprised that January wasn't fit for human consumption. It got so cold, all the people were bringing their brass monkeys into the house. And it stayed cold so long that Willie Onthenextranch had to change his long johns once.

But then February came along. We had a string of pretty days when the temperature climbed up into the 40s and 50s. The ice on the tanks melted down to a skim, and we had time to get all our windmills back together. It didn't even seem like winter any more.

Me and Willie were discussing the weather one day in February, over cups of his latest coffee substitute, Cambridge tea. Cambridge tea is a lot like hot coffee with cream and suger, but without the coffee. I could go a long time between cups of Cambridge tea, but I've got to admit that it was better than his sagebrush tea.

Willie was on a snort about weather forecasters. "They've started using these percentages now. Twenty per cent chance of snow! Now, what is a 20 per cent chance of snow? It's an 80 per cent chance of nuthin'. The odds are 4-to-1 that it ain't going to snow, so why do they even mention it?"

"Beats me," I said.

"Well I'll tell you why they do it. Forecasting the weather is show business. People don't watch the weather night after night just to hear 'fair to partly cloudy,' and them forecasters know it. If they don't come up with some bad weather now and then, they'll go out of business. And if that happened, they'd have to take an honest job.

"So what do they do? They talk about a 20 per cent chance of show. Now, how could you go wrong with a forecast like that? There's a 20 per cent chance that we'll get snow in July. There's a 20 per cent chance that all my cows will have donkeys instead of calves. There's a 20 per cent chance that anything will happen, and there's also a 20 per cent chance that nuthin' will happen—ever.

"The fact is, weather forecasters can't tell you anything except that we'll have weather of some kind tomorrow and Thursday, and maybe we'll have some more on the weekend. It's the only job in the world where a man can say nothing, repeat the obvious, and still draw a salary."

"What about politics?" I asked. He wasn't listening.

"And I'll tell you something else. Ranchers are the biggest saps in the world because, at 6:15 of an evening, every son-of-a-buck in this country is sitting in front of a TV set, watching the weather report. They used to say there's a sucker born every minute. A dozen would be closer to the truth."

About that time, Willie's wife drove in from town. She

said the whole town was talking about the big storm. "A blizzard's moving down from Canada," she said, "and it's supposed to hit us day after tomorrow."

Willie smirked. "You see? There's a blizzard in Canada. I bet there's even a typhoon in Japan, and a hail storm in Siberia. I guess we'd better take the rest of the week off."

Willie's a stubborn man. He'd convinced himself that nobody but a fool would watch the weather report, and after the news went off that evening, he got up and left the room. When Iris stayed up to watch the weather, he sneered at her and said she was a sap. But he didn't go too far away. In the next room he cocked his ear and listened. Sure enough, they were talking about a big blizzard. South Dakota was buried under a foot of snow, and the storm was moving south.

"Willie, you'd better come in here and listen to this."

He watched from the door but didn't sit down, since that would have violated his principles. Winter storm watch. Stockmen's warnings. Blizzard conditions. He switched the channel to get another report. Heavy snow and high winds for Thursday. He switched to another channel. More of the same. For once, all three forecasters were predicting a blizzard on the same day.

The next morning at sunrise, Willie started preparing for the storm. He fed all his cows three pounds of cottonseed instead of two. He drove into town and bought a set of snow chains for his pickup, a new pair of four-buckle overshoes and a pair of insulated gloves. On the way back to the ranch, he listened to the radio. The storm was supposed to hit about midnight.

He worked like a demon all afternoon. He went out on horseback and brought two thin cows to the house where he could give them extra feed. He hauled 50 bales of alfalfa over to the middle pasture. If worse came to worse, he could get over there on a horse and feed out of a sled. He drug the sled out of the barn and loaded it with three sacks of cake, and he left his horse in the corral instead of turning him out into the horse trap.

At 5 o'clock he caught the latest weather report on the radio. The blizzard was still moving south and getting worse by the hour.

Just to be on the safe side, he filled three cream cans with water and lugged them up to the porch. When Iris asked what he was doing, he said, "Honey, if this storm knocks out the electric, we'll be out of water. These things sometimes blow for days and days."

That night Willie was so restless he could hardly sit still. Every 15 minutes he got up and went outside to have a look. He checked the thermometer and studied the sky. It was clear and warm and quiet as death, a sure sign that a storm was moving in. At 10 o'clock he laid out his blizzard clothes by the door: one-piece long johns, wool socks, chaps, flannel shirt, insulated vest, leather coat, warm cap, neck scarf, lined gloves and overshoes. Everything was ready, so he went to bed.

But every time the clock chimed the hour he got up and checked the sky. At midnight there was still no sign of the storm. Then, around 3 o'clock, he heard the wind roaring like a locomotive. "There it is!" He jumped out of bed and ran to the window. The snow was so thick he couldn't even see the barn. He started pulling on his clothes. His wife asked him where on earth he was going at that hour. "Honey, this is going to be a bad one. I'd better go down and check those thin cows at the barn. We may be snowed in for a day or two."

Fighting against the wind and snow, he made his way down to the barn and threw half a bale of bright alfalfa hay into the pen with the cows. Before this thing blew over, they might need it.

Then, all at once, he straightened up and cocked his ear. The wind had died to a whisper. The snow had stopped. He looked up at the sky and saw the Big Dipper. And the Little Dipper. And the moon.

The storm was over. And there he was, feeding his cows at 3 o'clock in the morning. In his new gloves and overshoes. Beside the loaded feed sled.

Sap.

Christmas

I guess it was two days before Christmas. I drove into Alkali to get some windmill parts and to do a little last minute Christmas shopping, which seems to be the only kind I ever do. While I was in town, I figured I'd run out to the Alkali County Spearmint Station and see what old Barley McOatwheat was up to.

As usual, I slipped into the broom closet near the front door and peeked through the hole in the cinder-block wall. I do this to observe the great mind at work. Dr. McOatwheat was just coming out of his laboratory at the rear of the building and into the office, where Miss Mattie Sparrow sat at her desk sharpening pencils.

McOatwheat was wearing his usual: wrinkled suit coat, baggy pants, a yellowish-white shirt and a dusty bow tie. One shoe was untied and his socks didn't match. His gray hair was sticking out in all directions under his hat as though he had stuck a finger into a light socket. The expression on his face suggested that he was deep in thought; so deep, in fact, that he tripped on a throwrug and fell on the floor.

In the wink of an eye, Miss Mattie was beside him, wringing her hands. "Oh, Doctor, are you hurt? It's all my fault. I should know better that to put a rug in the middle of the room. I'm so sorry!" She helped him up and began slapping the dust off his clothes.

McOatwheat shrank back to escape the blows. "Control yourself, woman! Never mind the dust. I've got an idea and we must get it down on paper before it leaves me! Hurry, to your desk!"

Miss Mattie scrambled for her pad and pencil. "Ready for dictation, Doctor."

The scientist plunged his hands deep into his pants pockets, dropped his head almost to his chest and began pacing in front of the desk. "All right, Mattie, this one goes straight to Washington, a confidential report to be read only by the secretary of agriculture. Subject: Control of Skunkbrush in the Panhandle, and Perhaps the World.

"Dear Mr. Secretary: Scientists at Alkali County Experiment Station have just completed preliminary studies on a revolutionary method of controlling the deciduous pest known as skunkbrush. Under our hypothesis, skunkbrush plants can be rendered sterile in the laboratory and then transplanted in their native habitat. The sterile plants will cross-pollinate with others of the species, but the process will not result in the formation of seeds."

Waiting for Miss Mattie to catch up, McOatwheat pulled a red bandana from his hip pocket and blew his nose. Then he continued.

"This sterile plant will be a miracle of genetic research, produced by the crossing of skunkbrush plants with skunks."

Miss Mattie stopped writing and looked up. "Skunks?"

McOatwheat threw his hands into the air. "We have no time for discussion! Hurry, before the inspiration leaves me!"

She returned to her shorthand. "According to the hypothesis, animal characteristics will be dominant in the F-1 generation, but the F-2 crossing should produce a dendriform organism with black-and-white striped leaves and a powerful odor.

"It is our scientific opinion that this radical hypothesis could completely revolutionize mankind's approach to brush control. However." He stopped pacing and raised a bony finger in the air. "To continue this important research, we must have *funds* and *equipment* and *staff*! I respectfully request a grant of five hundred thousand dollars, etcetera, etcetera and etcetera, sincerely yours, Barley McOatwheat, PdQ."

He cut his eyes toward Miss Mattie, and seeing that she was still bent over her tablet, he sneaked the bottle out of his coat pocket and took a quick swallow. He gasped and fanned the vapors with his hand.

Miss Mattie's head came up and she sniffed the air. "Do I smell fruitcake?"

"Very likely, Mattie," he croaked, "this being the Christmas season. Which reminds me. You're leaving today to spend the holidays with your sister. You might as well go now. You deserve an extra hour of folly."

Miss Mattie heaved a sigh and gave him a troubled look. "But Doctor, what will you do? How will you spend the holiday?"

"Oh," he glanced away. "I'll manage, Mattie. The work of a scientist is never done, you know."

"But you'll be all alone . . . "

He finally had to order her out. She left reluctantly, casting glances over her shoulder. When the sound of her car disappeared in the distance, I crept out also, leaving Dr. McOatwheat standing alone in the empty building, his hands thrust into his pockets and both shoes untied.

Ten minutes later, I found Willie Onthenextranch at the pitch parlor and told him what I'd just heard. "I'll bet old Doc is going to spend Christmas all alone out there. That ain't right, Willie. Everybody deserves a happy Christmas."

Willie agreed, and it didn't take him long to come up with a scheme. The next day was Christmas Eve, and we spent most of it getting things ready. Around eight o'clock that evening we drove out to the Spearmint Station, both of us dressed in borrowed Santa Claus suits (except for our hats and boots) and carrying gunny sacks filled with candy, fruit cookies and Christmas pretties.

We wanted to surprise McOatwheat, so instead of knocking, we stood outside the door and started singing "Joy to the World." It was a little off-key, but plenty loud. We waited and waited. No one came to the door, so we sang it again, louder. Then the door opened a crack and out came McOatwheat's shotgun. I guess he thought we were hippies or something.

We talked him out of shooting us, and when he realized what we were doing, tears came to his eyes and he invited us in. We had brought a thermos of punch, and after washing down the trail dust, we went to work. Willie cut a big tumble-weed from the yard and brought it in. That was the Christmas tree, and we decorated it with paper, fruit, candy and whatever else we could find.

I took an old boot sock and wrote "DOC" on it with magic marker. We nailed it to the wall and filled it up with oranges and apples and hard candy. We hung candy canes on the windows and a paper angel over the door. When that was all done, we wished him a merry Christmas and said good night.

But Doc was having such a good time he didn't want us to leave. He just happened to have a little more punch on hand, and our throats just happened to be dry by then. After the punch had gone around several times, we started singing again. We sang old cowboy songs and Christmas carols, and then sang them again.

It was Doc who saw the woman standing in the doorway. He stopped singing. Then I stopped. Then Willie stopped. We all stared at the door.

59

G.L. Holmes

"Why Mattie," McOatwheat finally managed to say, and I guess that was all he could think of. Silence reigned.

I could see, from the angle of Miss Mattie's nose, that she had not come to join the party. She glared first at me, then at Willie and back to me again.

"Well, Doc," I said, clearing my throat, "I guess we'd better be getting along."

We went slinking to the door, with Miss Mattie blistering us with her stare. As we passed her, she said, "The very idea! Two grown men dressing up like ragamuffins and disturbing the sleep of an important scientist!"

We made a hurried exit. Outside we heard Miss Mattie say that she had worried all day about Dr. McOatwheat, so she had brought her sister back to Alkali, and they would all spend Christmas day at her house. Then she said, in a low voice, "I think those men had been drinking, Doctor."

"Very likely, Mattie," he said. "It's unfortunate but true that we live in a world of low moral standards."

"I knew I shouldn't have left you," she sighed. "Something always seems to happen."

"So it seems, Mattie. As the philosopher said, 'Vigilance is . . . something or other.' In any case, you always seem to rescue me just in the nick of time. Another minute, and they might have forced liquor upon me."

"And then," Miss Mattie replied in a louder voice, "I would have been forced to wring a few cowboy necks!"

We hustled to the pickup, neither of us wanting a broken neck for Christmas. As we drove off, Willie leaned out the window and yelled, "Merry Christmas to all, and to all a good night!" Then, in an aside, he added, "You psalm-singing old battle-ax."

The Super Boil

Willie Onthenextranch takes his football seriously, especially when it comes to the Dallas Cowboys.

He can't sit down during a game. He gets right up in front of the television and cheers the boys on. "Come on, Harvey! Go get 'em. Too Tall! Sic 'em, Randy! When the Cowboys lose, Willie's mood goes rancid for several days. When they win, he becomes almost bearable.

He had a tough season last year. In mid-season, when it appeared the Cowboys would fumble themselves into oblivion, he disowned the team and switched his heart and soul to the Houston Oilers.When Houston was thrashed by Pittsburgh in the play-offs, he suffered heartburn and spiritual decline, and disavowed them.

A week before Super Bowl day, he was once again a loyal Dallas fan. There was no more talk about the Oilers. Willie's version of the season was that he had singlehandedly turned the Cowboys around by threatening to support another team. He also gave some credit to Tom Landry.

Willie was counting the days to Super Bowl Sunday, and

he had his work all planned out. He would double-feed on Monday, so that on Sunday he would just have to do chores. He and I agreed to watch the game together. It was all set.

And then, around daylight Sunday morning, it began to snow. By noon it was five degrees and still snowing. Not only would Willie have to feed, but he would have to feed hay, which took more time than sacked feed.

He bundled up and pulled on his four buckle overshoes and got right down to the most important business of the day—he stepped outside and screamed at the clouds.

Then he ran to his pickup. If he hurried, he would have just enough time to make his feed run and get back to the house in time for the opening kickoff. He could listen to the pre-game show on the pickup radio.

He put the pickup in four-wheel drive and roared off to the stack lot, sending snow in all directions. The stack lot was located in a trap behind the house, where he was wintering a small bunch of old, thin cows. There wasn't a cow in sight when he pulled up to the gate. Since he was in a hurry, he threw the gate back and left it down.

He backed up to the stack and started slinging bales into the pickup. When he stopped for a breath of air five minutes later, he saw that every cow in the pasture was standing in the gate, bawling and staring with bovine stupidity at the stack of delicious alfalfa hay.

He didn't have time to shut the gate, then open it, then shut it again. "Git outa here!" he yelled. If he hurried, he could get out of the stack lot before they came in. He started slinging bales. When he looked up again, 15 cows had come through the gate and were heading for the stack.

In fury, he jumped to the ground, seized a piece of windmill rod, and attacked. The cows bolted and ran out the gate, all but one skinny wretch, who ran around to the back side of the stack. Willie chased her around the stack three times, threatening to cut her throat and feed her to the maggots. Finally she left, and Willie had to shut the gate anyway.

He was running late now, and he worked like a demon to get the hay loaded. Since he intended to make only one trip to the east pastures, he had to get 40 bales on the pickup.

He drove to the gate, drove out, shut the fool gate, and headed east. The pickup rocked back and forth, and he waited for the load to fall. It stayed. He snapped on the radio and tuned in the pre-game show. He had to hurry.

He made it to the east pasture and drove to the feed ground, honking and bawling as he drove. Ten cows were waiting on the feed ground, 10 out of 125. He honked and bawled, honked and bawled. The pre-game show came on.

He drummed his fingers on the steering wheel. He could see the rest of the cows. They were standing on the other side of a draw, mooing in the snow. They wanted breakfast in bed.

"Well that's tough!" he yelled out the window. "You want grub, you come get it. We ain't giving room service today."

He waited. The cows didn't move. He honked, they bellered. He swore, they mooed. The pre-game show came to an end. Kickoff was in five minutes. Well, that didn't change anything. Willie fed his cattle *on the feed ground*. That was a matter of principle. He wasn't going to compromise, even if he had to miss seeing part of the Super Bowl.

The cows on the feed ground began eating the hay on the pickup. All at once, the top-most bale slid off, crashed on top of the cab, bounced down on the hood, and broke off the radio antenna.

The Super Bowl broadcast, which was about to begin, went dead.

Willie threw the pickup into gear and spun off toward the cows on the other side of the draw. To hell with principle, this was an emergency!

There was only one good and quick way to unload the

hay. Put the pickup in compound and let her go, while he got in the back and threw off the bales. With this big a load, there were some risks involved, but he didn't have time to nickle and dime the bales, not on Super Bowl day.

He threw her into compound and hopped out. Climbing up the stack proved no easy task, and by the time he crawled to the top, the pickup had already traveled 200 feet, and had come upon some rough ground. The hay lurched back and forth. Willie dropped to his hands and knees and held on for dear life.

The wheels hit a huge frozen cow pile, and old Willie

G.L. Holmes

knew it was all over. He and the bale he was clinging to went over the side, and the rest of the load came right behind him.

He was buried under 40 bales of alfalfa, while the pickup went merrily along in four-wheel drive compound. Heading for the creek.

Willie was covered with bales, and the bales were soon covered with hungry cows. Willie screamed and kicked and finally dug his way out, punching two cows in the nose in the process.

Free at last, he set out at a run, puffing through the snow in his four-buckle overshoes, to catch his wandering pickup. He caught it just in time—just in time to watch it go over a four-foot bank and settle into the creek.

But Willie was a determined man. He calculated that if he walked fast, he could make it home in time to see most of the second half. Off he went.

An hour later, sweating and drenched with snow, he flew into the house and yelled, "Turn on the TV, Iris, my Dallas Cowboys need me!"

Iris emerged from the kitchen, wearing a puzzled grin. "Why, didn't you know, dear? The electricity went off right after you left."

Willie's eyes bulged. "What! After I . . . They can't do this to me! I'll sue the . . . gimme the phone!" He stomped to the phone. When he put it to his ear, he heard a familiar drone. It was dead. He flung the receiver into the trash and screamed, "They can't do this to me!"

"Now Willie, maybe we can play cards."

He stared at her and said, "Play cards. You don't understand. Nobody understands. I hate the electric company. I hate the phone company. I hate my cows. I hate. . . ."

He wandered out of the room, put on his pajamas, and went to bed.

Right to Work

Stopped in to see Willie Onthenextranch the other day. The price of coffee was still going up, so I didn't expect to get a cup. Willie had been serving sassafras tea to visitors since the first of the year, and I'd just about adjusted to it. But I guess the price of sassafras roots went up, so he quit buying that too.

He gave me a cup of sagebrush tea. "This stuff," he explained, "is made from natural, organically grown herbs that come off this very ranch. I made it myself, and I'll guarantee that it don't contain any caffeine, nicotine, soybean filler or plastic."

He went back to writing a letter at the kitchen table. I took one whiff of that sagebrush tea and got up to "stretch my legs." While Willie was biting the end of his pencil and scowling at the wall, I dumped the tea in with a potted plant. It looked like it needed watering anyway.

(Two days later, that plant was dead.)

"What you writing, Willie?" I asked, easing back into my chair.

He saw my empty cup. "You like that tea, huh?"

"I feel better already. What you writing?"

He folded his arms across his chest and leaned back in his chair. "I'm writing the President of the United States to let him know that I agree a hundred per cent with his secretary of labor. I think we ought to throw out these Right to Work Laws."

Well, that came as a real shock to me. I'd never met a cow chaser who was against Right to Work laws. "How come, Willie?"

"Can't you figger it out? I don't want to work, and I think I've got a constitutional right not to work. Is there any place in the Constitution where it says a man has to work for a living?" I said I guessed there wasn't. "Well, there you are. A man has to stand up for his rights. I've got a right to loaf if I want to, and I'm prepared to take it to court."

"Now wait a minute," I said. "If they repeal the Right to Work laws, we'll all have to join a labor union. I know for a fact that you've spent half your life cussing labor unions."

He shrugged. "That was before I'd give it much thought. I've decided it might be a good deal."

I argued at him for 15 minutes, telling him all the reasons why labor unions would destroy agriculture. He listened without comment or expression. When I ran out of breath, he said, "All right, are you finished? Then shut up and listen. You might learn something for a change.

"Now lookie here. Back East, you have a business and a labor force, two different outfits. Business wants low wages and high profits, and labor wants low profits and high wages. Naturally they're going to be at odds all the time.

"But now you take a small ranch like this one of mine. I'm owner and the manager and the hired hand, all rolled into one. If they repeal the Right to Work laws and my labor force has to join a union, who's that going to be?" He tapped himself on the chest. "Me."

"I still don't get it."

"Be patient, son," Willie said. "There's wisdom in this world if you'll just learn to wait. With the union behind me, I can demand better working conditions. Building fences and fixing windmills in the summer are going to be out. Too danged hot. Riding pastures and fixing windmills in the winter will be out. Too danged cold. Loading cows, moving bulls around and breaking horses won't be in my contract. Too dangerous.

"All heifers will have to calve between 9 and 5 o'clock on pretty days in the months of April or May. I'll have to have a new pickup to drive, with a stereo and a mobile phone. Any time I touch a bale of hay or a sack of feed, I want extra pay. When I weld, I want welder's wages. When I pick up a hammer, I want carpenter's wages. When I fool with a pump or a septic tank, I want plumber's wages. When I doctor a sick calf, there's going to be a vet fee. And every time I check the oil in the pickup, it's going to cost somebody 10 bucks an hour—and I'll make sure it takes an hour too."

"Now Willie. . . "

"I'll ask for a guaranteed wage of about two thousand a month, with six weeks' paid vacation and a month off for Christmas and a week off for Washington's birthday. As a compromise, I'll agree to work on Valentine's Day. Just in case the cattle market comes up, I'll want a profit sharing plan, with a jumpship clause in case the market goes down. See, I want money, not risk."

"Willie. . . "

"I want my health insurance paid by the company and I'm going to fight for a good pension plan—retirement at, oh, 40 years of age, drawing a thousand a month, plus vacation, plus housing allowance, plus beef and milk and eggs and a garden, and, of course, that'll all be tied to an inflation clause."

"Willie. . . "

"And if management don't agree to this contract, we'll

have to go on strike. We'll have a one month minimum on all strikes, and we'll want to draw half-pay and extra beef. And we'll need to use the company pickup so we can drive to town for food stamps and unemployment benefits." He scratched his head. "I guess that about covers it. Oh yeah, the company will have to put a coffee pot down at the barn and furnish the coffee."

I glared at him for half a minute. "Willie, that's the craziest thing I ever heard in my life. You'd be working against yourself."

"That's right! If I'm labor and management both, one of us is bound to come out ahead on the deal." He winked at me. "That's called hedging in a profit."

"No," I said "it's called ignorance and stupidity. You know as well as I do that it won't work. Eventually somebody has to pay the bills. You can't make all those demands on a cattle ranch that was losing money to start with."

"No?" he grinned. "What makes you think so?"

"Well. . . Willie, you old goat, stop talking that way! If the company's broke, it's broke, and it can't go on hiring people and paying wages. Anybody knows that."

He shook his head. "You don't read the papers do you? Listen, the courts of these United States have already ruled that a company can't lay off workers just because it's losing money, because that would deny the workers their civil rights. My ranch has to hire me and pay my wages whether it wants to or not, and whether it's making money or not. That's the law."

"That may be the law," I yelled, "but who's going to pay the bills, and where's the money going to come from!"

He picked his teeth for a minute. "That's what's known as a legal technicality, and my union ain't going to mess with legal technicalities. The government bailed out New York, let 'em bail out my ranch. It ain't my problem. All I know is that I've got my rights and I want my money." He gave me another wink. "I've got 'em licked this time, brother. All these years I've been telling you that a man could make money in the cattle business. Well, this is it. We just have to work both sides of the street."

I guess you never know till you try.

OSHA

I happened to be at the Alkali Post Office one day last month looking through several days' accumulation of third class mail, when I saw a man trying to get in the front door. It was Dr. Barley McOatwheat, resident scientist at the Spearmint Station.

I couldn't remember seeing McOatwheat at the post office before, and the longer I watched him the more I understood why Miss Mattie was usually the one who picked up the mail.

As I say, he was trying to get in the front door. He pushed on the door, and he pushed and he pushed, and right beside his hand was a big red sign that said, in English, PULL. After struggling for several minutes, he threw up his hands and walked away, muttering under his breath. Just then, a little girl about 10 years old walked up to the door, pulled it open and came inside.

McOatwheat observed this with a sour expression,

glanced over both shoulders to see if anyone had been watching him, then entered the post office as though he had been doing it every day of his life.

He went straight to his box and pulled out a key ring that must have had 25 or 30 keys on it. At a distance, I guessed that it held every key to every padlock, suitcase and automobile he had owned over the past 50 years. He scowled at the keys, mumbled something to himself, and then began trying every key in the lock. This must have gone on for 15 or 20 minutes.

Finally one of the keys slid into the lock, but apparently he didn't push it in far enough. He tried to turn it to the left. He tried to turn it to the right. He jiggled it up and down. His face turned red and his eyes began to bulge. He jiggled it again, then pounded on the box with his fist. The key still wouldn't turn in the lock.

Then he seized the ring with both hands and pulled with all his might, and that fixed it. The key broke off in the lock.

The postmaster had to get his mail out of the box, and 30 minutes after he had entered the building, McOatwheat finally made it to one of the tables to sort through his mail. By then I had trashed all mine and went over to say hello. He was reading a letter so intently that he barely managed to grumble a greeting. I happened to glance at the letterhead and saw that it was from OSHA, a rather unpopular federal agency in our end of the country. Naturally I was curious, so I read over his shoulder.

The letter said that OSHA was funding research projects on occupational hazards in the cattle business. If Dr. McOatwheat would care to submit a proposal, the agency would consider funding his research.

The talk around town was that McOatwheat and the Spearmint Station had been on the brink of financial catastrophe for a long time. The station was supported by federal money, but it had never amounted to much, and some people believed that Mattie Sparrow had been subsidizing McOatwheat's research for years.

In the meantime, he had concocted an endless procession of crackpot schemes and had sent countless proposals to government agencies and private foundations in the hope of getting a research grant that would solve all his money problems.

So when he read the letter from OSHA, he was practically beside himself with joy. I tried to make conversation, and even walked him out to his old Hudson Hornet (which had come to rest with one wheel over the curb), but by then his wonderful intelligence had moved on to a higher plane and I couldn't get a word out of him. He jumped into the Hornet, gunned the motor, looked back over his shoulder and came close to driving through the front wall of the post office. In his excitement, he had forgotten to put the car in reverse.

You can understand why McOatwheat was excited. If there was ever a federal agency that could put his ideas to good use it was OSHA. He went into seclusion for five days and gave Miss Mattie strict orders to turn away visitors and refuse all phone calls (he needn't have bothered, since there were none anyway). While she kept him alive with sandwiches and soup and little bowls of stewed prunes, McOatwheat directed his brilliance like a laser beam toward the problem of occupational hazards in the cow business.

On the afternoon of the fifth day, he burst out of his laboratory and thundered into the office where Miss Mattie had dozed off at her desk. "Mattie, I've got it, I'm ready! It's all here in this wonderful brain! Prepare for dictation!"

Mattie awakened with a start, just in time to see Dr. McOatwheat trip over an extension cord and fall into a large trash can near the back door. Even in the trash can, he continued to thrust his right index finger into the air in a gesture of triumph. His eyes were red behind his spectacles, his hair in wild disarray. When she had gotten him out of the can, he did not thank her, but bellowed, "To your desk, Mattie! Quickly, quickly, before the inspiration vanishes like the morning dew!" In an instant, she was at her desk and ready to write.

Hands clasped behind his back, McOatwheat paced the office with long restless strides. "The question before us today is one of utmost importance: Is it true that today's ranching operations are hazardous and dangerous to human beings? The answer is an unequivocal yes. Let us consider the following specific examples.

"Ordinary tank water can be a killer. Recent studies show that if tank water is breathed for periods of up to five

G.L. Holmes

minutes, it can have a toxic effect on the respiratory system. The respiring of water is a major cause of drowning in America; stock tanks are the primary repository of water on our nation's ranches; therefore, stock tanks create a deadly and intolerable hazard to all organisms which might attempt to breathe the water therein. Any substance which can cause death is, by definition, poisonous. Hence, by simple logic, we reach 'the astounding conclusion that tank water is poisonous.''

That is an astounding conclusion!'' said Miss Mattie.

"Yes, isn't it." He stared at her. "Mattie, is that a tarantula on the wall behind you?" Miss Mattie shrieked and turned to the wall, while McOatwheat whipped out his bottle of sagebrush thinner and took several swallows. "I was mistaken," he choked. "Back to dictation.

"Barbed wire is another dangerous substance. In studies conducted at the Alkali Experiment Station, laboratory animals were fed a regular diet of barbed wire. Our data have shown that, if consumed in large quantities, barbed wire can produce malnutrition, bleeding ulcers and fatuous quadrivalence of the jowl. It may be premature at this point to say that barbed wire is poisonous, but that conclusion is certainly indicated by the data.''

McOatwheat tapped his toe as he waited for Miss Mattie to catch up. Then he plunged on. "We have not had the opportunity to test other substances under laboratory conditions, but it is our opinion that they too should be regarded as dangerous. Dehorning tubes, drill bits and welding rods should never be eaten. Not only can they interfere with the normal digestive functions, but they can also produce broken mandibles.''

"Broken what?" Mattie asked.

"Jaws, Mattie. We would issue the same caution about galvanized pipe, vaccinating needles, nose tongs and certain varieties of nylon rope. We strongly advise ranchers and their employees to refrain from eating these products until further research has been conducted.

"In conclusion, our preliminary investigations have indicated that ranch work and equipment may pose such an overwhelming hazard to human health and safety that further research is not only advisable, but it would be criminal not to pursue it at once. However . . . " Up came the index finger. "We must have *funds* and *equipment* and *staff*! I should think that a grant in the amount of $800,000 would be sufficient, Sincerely yours, Barley McOatwheat, PdQ." When Mattie had finished her dictation, he said, "Well, what do you think?"

She sighed and placed both hands over her heart. "Oh Doctor, you're just brilliant! Taking down your words for posterity is an honor, and I only hope that I am worthy of it."

For a long time the scientist said nothing, as his eyes seemed fixed on some distant point. Finally he spoke. "What can I say, Mattie? Once again your simple words have exposed a shining truth. But let us never forget that it was your egg salad sandwiches that made it all possible."

The Bargain Horse

Several weeks ago Willie Onthenextranch and I went to the livestock auction in Alkali. The day was bright and cool, fall grass was looking pretty good, cattle prices were holding and everyone was in a happy mood. I felt so good, I bought Willie a piece of raisin pie and a cup of coffee. He didn't thank me, but he burped several times, and I figured that he enjoyed it.

We talked around and caught up on all that gossip until the jackpot sale started, then we went into the barn and took our seats. After they ran the jackpot stuff and the baby calves, in came a big black gelding with a 10-year old boy in the saddle.

"Boys," said the auctioneer, "if you've been looking for a

nice saddlehorse to take back to the country, here he is. He's gentle enough for this boy to ride, and we've got the papers to go with him. All he needs is a home. Start him at a thousand."

He didn't get any takers at a thousand, so he came down to seven six-bits. Nobody bid. He stopped and lectured us about how we all needed this horse and how he wasn't going to give him away. "Remember, boys, the papers go with him." But he dropped the bid down to five hundred. He still didn't get any takers, and it made him so mad that he dropped it down to a hundred dollars. All at once the crowd woke up and hands started flying through the air.

I noticed that one of those hands belonged to Willie Onthenextranch.

"Say," I whispered, "you're not thinking of buying that horse, are you?"

The bid was up around a hundred and seventy by then. "No, I ain't going to buy him." he said with a wicked gleam in his eye. "I'm gonna steal him."

The auctioneer called for two-fifty. Willie jerked his head and stayed in the running.

"Willie," I said, "let me tell you something about that horse."

"Will you shut your yap? How can I steal a horse with you talking in my ear?"

He bought the gelding for three hundred bucks. The little boy cried as he pulled the saddle and bridle. The auctioneer moaned and howled about what a bunch of tightwads we were for letting such a fine registered horse—and a little boy's pet—go for a paltry $300. Willie lapped up every word, and by the time the papers were passed through the crowd and reached his hands, he was swollen up like a toad.

He couldn't have been happier if he had just cheated a widow out of her last quarter.

He cocked his hat back on his head and turned to me with an arrogant little smirk on his mouth. "Registered. Geld-

79

ing. Kid gentle. Three hundred bucks. Fifty years ago, they would have hung me for a horse thief. Now, what was it you were fixin' to tell me?"

"Nuthin'. You don't want to hear it."

"Well, I ain't going to beg, but if you've got something to say, I'll sure hear you out before I tell you how wrong you are. Go ahead."

"You just bought yourself a lemon."

He chuckled. "When you've been around horses as long as I have, you'll want to buy that kind of lemon by the dozen. You may not know it, but good horses these days are bringing a thousand bucks and more."

"Uh huh, but that's good horses, Willie. Did you happen to notice who was bidding against you on that horse? Three packer buyers. Why do you suppose nobody but the packers wanted him?"

That didn't upset him at all, and he gave another chuckle. "Everybody else was asleep and the horse just slipped through. That's when you get the real bargains." He aimed a finger at me. "Write this down in your little notebook: Any time you can pick up a usin' horse at a packer price, you've beat the system."

"All right," I said. "Now you write this down in your little notebook: A cheap horse is a cheap horse; you get just what you pay for."

"Oh yeah? Well let me tell you something else. It'll be a cold day in hell when I pay more than $300 for a saddlehorse. I never have, and I ain't startin' now."

"And that," I said, "explains why you have Alkali County's most complete collection of nags, broncs and broomtails. Willie, you've only got one horse that's fit to ride, and he's so ugly I wouldn't ride him through the desert on a dark night. Why don't you just break down and buy yourself a good saddlehorse?"

He glared at me. "That's what I just did. The only bad

thing you can say about that horse is that he didn't cost enough money."

"No, as a matter of fact, that's not what bothers me at all. What bothers me is that I've seen that same gelding go through this sale ring three times in the past six months. Does that tell you anything?"

He gave me his stubborn look. "What do you want the poor horse to do, refuse to walk through the ring? Go on strike? Get a court injunction? Is it the fault of the horse if someone wants to sell him?"

"Willie, I think you missed the point."

"No, I got the point. The point is that I can judge a good horse when I see one, and that is a good horse. He's sound, he's put together right, he's gentle, he's papered, and he came through the sale ring with a 10-year-old kid on his back. You were so busy worrying about the low price that you didn't notice that the kid cried when he pulled off the saddle for the last time. Cried. Now, that's the kind of sign a shrewd buyer looks for. It tells you a lot more about the horse than the price tag does."

I smiled. "All right, Willie, I guess you've got me there."

"You bet I do. See, kids don't lie."

"No, they sure don't, Willie."

"That was the tip-off. You have to keep your eyes open at these sales."

"Uh huh."

"Watch for the little signs. They'll tell you what you need to know."

"I see. Well, all I can say is that you're a shrewd man."

Willie laughed. "Oh, you nailed me there! Shrewd and cold-blooded and heartless in a horse deal. Yup, that's me."

"I'd sure like to be around when you take that horse out the first time."

He whopped me on the back. "Well by Ned, let's go do it!"

I sure was looking forward to that. Since Willie was so shrewd, I didn't bother to tell him that that 10-year old kid was the son of a horse trader, that he'd played that crying scene in every sale ring from Amarillo to Dodge City, and that he was the same as a professional actor. The sorrier the horse, the harder he cried.

Maybe Willie was right that kids didn't lie, but this one sure could give a false impression.

Willie paid for the horse and we led him to the trailer. He stepped right up and went to the front. Willie beamed. "You think a thousand dollar horse could load any better than that?"

All the way out to the ranch, he was grinning and talking to himself. "Three hundred bucks! Boy, I stole their bacon and eggs today. They may never let me back in that sale barn. Heh, heh. Did you see that auctioneer's face? There for a minute, I thought he was going to pack up and go home. Heh, heh."

"Heh, heh," I echoed.

At the ranch, we unloaded the horse and led him to Willie's saddle room. Willie saddled him up and tightened the cinch. The horse didn't even bat an eye. Willie grinned and climbed on and started putting the horse through his paces. He walked him, he trotted him, he loped him around the pen. I had to admit the horse moved well and looked good. Next, Willie reined him: left, right, left, right. The horse had good action, and Willie was almost beside himself.

"Look at that! I believe he's been trained as a cutting horse. Ha, ha! You see what three hundred bucks will buy? No wonder that kid was bawling."

"You really skinned him, Willie."

He said he wanted to take the horse out into the pasture and rope a calf or two. "If he's got some roping sense, I'll bet I can sell him tomorrow to some of them team ropers for $800."

We loaded the horse into the trailer again and drove out into the pasture. By this time, Willie was almost unbearable. I was able to stand him only because I had a gut feeling that the

moment of judgment was yet to come. We drove up to a
windmill and stopped. Willie unloaded the horse and climbed
on. "Five hundred bucks profit ain't bad wages for a cowboy."
He spurred the horse and loped toward the cattle around the
windmill.

Then it happened. When the horse saw the cattle, he
came to a sudden stop. His ears shot up, his eyes got as big as
saucers and his nostrils flared. One old cow took a step toward
him. The horse bogged his head, wheeled around, and headed
for the barn as fast as he could go—which wasn't too fast since
he was bucking every third step. Willie lost his hat on the first
jump, one stirrup on the second, the other stirrup on the third,
the saddle horn on the fourth and his horse on the fifth. He did
one of the prettiest swan dives I ever saw, then nosed into a
sandhill. The horse went to the house.

I picked up Willie's hat and walked over to where he'd

G.L. Holmes

bedded down. He had sand all over his face and murder in his eyes. "Willie, it appears to me your horse might be a little bashful around cattle." He snatched the hat out of my hand. "But he might be real good around prairie dogs." He stomped toward the pickup. "And if you ever needed to sort up a load of jackrabbits. . . . " We got into the pickup and Willie spun the tires for a hundred yards. "Well, one thing about it, Willie. We know the horse is gentle around kids. Why, I'll bet even a 10-year old kid could ride him."

That got him. He swung his eyes around and curled his lip. "That just tells you what this world is coming to. Everybody's out for the almighty dollar, even the dad-danged kids."

"That's right, Willie. The world's going to pot."

He glared at me. "Are you makin' fun of me?"

"Who me?"

"Well, let me give you one piece of advice."

"Never buy a cheap horse?"

"Drop dead."

Willie's Heifers

Couple of weeks ago I finished my feed run and thought I'd drop by and see Willie Onthenextranch. Instead of knocking at the back door, I just walked in.

There sat old Willie at the kitchen table. He was humped over a calculator and chewing on the end of a pencil. He had a bunch of papers spread out in front of him. He was so deep in concentration that at first he didn't hear me come in.

Now, if he'd just looked up and said howdy and told me he was working on his income tax, I wouldn't have thought anything about it. But that's not what he did. When he saw me, he reacted like a kid who's just been caught chewing tobacco behind the chicken house.

In a flash, he gathered up all those pieces of paper and stuffed them into a folder. While he was doing this, he asked, "What's the weather supposed to do?" I didn't answer. He started whistling and backed up to the table and slipped the calculator into his pocket. "Sure looks like snow to me," he said.

85

The sun was shining outside.

Well, Willie was up to something. I didn't know what it was, but since he was acting so silly about it, I decided to find out.

"What you been doing this morning, Willie?"

"Me? Oh nuthin. Just the same old nuts and bolts."

"What was that you slipped into your hip pocket?"

"Huh? What hip pocket?"

"Looked like a calculator to me."

"Oh that."

I waited for him to say more. He didn't. "And what were those papers you didn't want me to see?"

"What papers?"

"Willie, you old rip, what are you up to? You look like you've spent all morning trying to figure out how to cheat a widow woman out of some money."

His face fell and he gave me a hard look. "Who told?"

That business about the widow woman had been a shot in the dark, but danged if that wasn't exactly what he'd been doing. I finally got the story out of him.

Seems there was a poor old widow woman over in the next county who had a nice set of pregnant heifers, and Willie was trying to talk her into selling them. He'd told her how much trouble first-calf heifers were and had offered, "as a personal favor," to take them off her hands.

The rest of the plan, which he hadn't mentioned to her, was that he would hold them for four months, calve them out, sell them as pairs and make a tub-full of money on them.

By the time he had finished telling me this, his eyes were glittering like diamonds and he was rubbing his hands together.

"That sounds mighty good," I said, "but you've got to calve them out first. Like you told her, heifers are a mess."

Willie snorted. "That's my trump card. The old biddy let it slip out that them heifers was all bred to calve in March, and

86

they're all bred to Red Razorback bulls." He waited for me to say something. I just gave him my usual dumb expression. "Red Razorback bulls, in case you don't know, throw the smallest calf in the world. You never have calving problems. You can throw your pulling chains away. A heifer spits that red calf out like a watermelon seed."

"I didn't know that."

"Neither does the old lady. I'll take delivery in January, watch 'em calve out in March, sell 'em in April when the spring market starts up."

"Well," I said, "you've sure got it figgered. I just hope you can live with your conscience, taking advantage of that poor widow woman."

Willie assumed a pose of mock-sorrow. "It'll be tough, but I think I can manage."

He took delivery on the heifers on New Year's Day and put them in a trap south of the house. On Jan. 2 a norther roared in and it started snowing. A week later, when I stopped in at his place, it was colder than a well-digger. Willie wasn't at the house, so I went down to the corral.

Right off, I saw that old Willie had bought himself a wreck. That bunch of heifers, bred to calve "in March," had started going off like a box full of loaded mousetraps.

Willie was standing behind the cow chute, staring with bleary eyes at two little yellow hooves and a tongue coming out of a straining heifer. He had two more heifers lined up in the alley. Out in the trap, I could see three more walking around with their tails out.

His pens were filled with the heifers he had already calved out. He had adoptions working on three. Another had thrown her womb, and he'd worked the old pop-bottle-and-stitch treatment on her. Four more heifers had rejected their calves and were wearing hobbles on their back legs. Another was paralyzed and had to be milked out, and her calf fed from a nipple bottle.

G.L.Holmes

If I had owned any Red Razorback bulls, I would have gone right home and cut their throats.

"Hi Willie," I sang out. "How's everything going?"

He beamed me a murderous glare from his bloodshot eyes. "How do you think everything is going? Does it look like me and the polar bears are out here watchin' the rory-bory-alice?"

I studied the situation. "No. It looks to me like this is March already and your heifers have started calving. I guess you didn't throw away your pulling chains."

"Very funny. Well let me tell you something." He made a pistol of his finger and aimed it at me. "That old bag lied and cheated me on these diddly-danged heifers. I dealt with her in good faith. I tried to do her a favor. I made an honest effort to help out an old woman in distress. You can see what it got me. Do you realize what this means?"

"Let's see." I scratched my head and thought for a minute. "It means you won't be going to the pool hall this month."

"No, that ain't what it means. It means that the morality of this country has hit rock bottom. You know what they say about the fall of the Roman Empire, don't you? Rome fell when they couldn't trust the widow women any more. So there you are."

"No kidding," I said. "I never heard that one before, Willie. Well, look at the bright side. If the country falls in the next week or two, maybe it'll fall on these heifers and you won't have to fool with them anymore."

Willie's eyes narrowed and he pointed his finger-pistol at me again. "I think you're trying to be funny."

"Who me?"

"At the very moment when this great nation of ours is on the brink of disaster, you're trying to be cute. Well, all I have to say to you, mister, is that down deep in your heart, where it really counts, you're a slob and a Communist."

I held up my hands in surrender. "Hold on, Willie, you've got it all wrong. I think it's very serious."

"Huh. Well, that's more like it."

"I mean, you got hustled by a little old lady and here you are freezing to death. How could there be anything ho ho funny about that ha ha?"

I knew he'd kill me if he ever got hold of me, but I couldn't stop laughing.

"It's just tee hee terrible!"

Willie's eyes burst into flames. Smoke poured out of his nostrils. He vaulted over the fence and came after me. "How would you like to have this pulling chain wrapped around your guzzle!" he screeched.

I headed for the pickup. "No thanks, I've got to fix some fence this afternoon." I dived into the pickup and started off. "Happy heifers, Willie!"

You know what he said then.

Mrs. Grundy's Hay

Willie Onthenextranch had an especially bad winter this year. If you recall, back in January he bought a nice set of springing heifers from a poor old widow woman named Mrs. Grundy.

He bought them cheap and was very proud of himself, but by the time he got them calved out and sold, he had managed to lose a lot of time and a tidy sum of money.

Well, on a warm spring day several weeks ago, I stopped by Willie's place to see if he was still licking his wounds after the heifer deal. He was on the phone, so I just walked in and helped myself to coffee. I was sitting at the kitchen table when he hung up.

Then I heard him laugh. That was odd.

When he came striding into the kitchen, he was grinning from ear to ear. "Oh what a wonderful day! Revenge, sweet revenge!"

I blew on my coffee and took a swig. It tasted like dishwater. Willie must have used the same coffee grounds four days in a row. "What's up?" I asked.

He stared at my cup. "Did you get that out of the coffee pot?" I nodded. "It's dishwater. Iris decided to soak the pot this morning."

"Oh." I put down the cup. "I thought it tasted a little worse than usual. So what are you grinning about?"

He flopped down into a chair and clasped his hands behind his neck. "That was Mrs. Grundy on the phone."

"The widow woman?"

"The same old bat who sold me them dad-danged heifers. She's out of feed, out of hay, and out of grass, and she wondered if I could sell her some good alfalfa hay."

"And?"

"And I said I'd just be glad to sell her a bobtail load for 3 bucks a bale."

"Well, that sounds good."

"Delivered."

"That doesn't sound so good."

"And you're gonna help."

"That sounds awful. I'd better be going." I got up and started for the door. I've got hay fever, the kind that makes me run at the very mention of hard work. But Willie caught me by th arm and wouldn't let go.

"Now hold on. I need your help. It's just one load and it won't be bad. Be a good neighbor."

"But I. . . "

"And just think: you'll have the pleasure of my company all day."

I stared at him. "Well, how could I turn down a deal like that? Gee, I'm honored, Willie."

"You should be. Come on, let's go."

We walked down to the barn and fired up his old bobtail truck. And I mean we *fired* it up, literally. A mouse had built a nest on the exhaust manifold and we were in flames before we got to the cattleguard. We got the fire beat out and drove to the stack lot.

Willie backed up to a stack that had been there for 5 years. You couldn't have found any sorrier hay if you'd looked for 2 weeks.

"You're selling Mrs. Grundy *this* hay for 3 bucks a bale? Why, this wouldn't even make good garden mulch."

"Tough. That old bag snookered me on them heifers, now I'm gonna snooker her on this hay. Revenge."

When I picked up the first bale, I knew why he had priced the hay by the bale instead of by the ton. Those bales weighed about 30 pounds apiece. The outside was bleached and stemmy, the inside was rotten. Most of them only had one wire left.

We went to work and started stacking. When we got up five high on the truck, I stopped and studied the load.

"Willie, these bales are awful cushy. Maybe we'd better not go any higher."

"We're going eight high, even if it takes a mile of rope to tie it down. I want revenge."

So we went eight high, and when we got done it looked like we had a truck load of feathers. "Willie, we'll never make it."

"Sure we will. It ain't but 15 miles. Revenge!" He rubbed his hands together. "I love it."

We ran two ropes from front to back, then two more ropes from side to side. We squeezed her down with the wire stretchers, hopped into the truck, and off we went.

When you live around Willie for a while, you learn to expect disaster. I figured the load of hay would ride for about a mile and a half, then we'd dump it on the cattle guard in the west pasture.

But I was wrong. Somehow it stayed on the truck and we made it to the highway.

"Well, we've got it made now," said Willie. "It's all

highway from now on. Hot dog! Let's see, 30 bales to the tier, 8 tiers, that's 240 bales at $3.00. $720. That ain't bad wages for garden mulch."

He whistled and hummed all the way. I watched the load in the side mirror. I kept waiting to see it fly apart, but somehow it stayed in one piece.

Mrs. Grundy lived in a little white house about 200 yards off the pavement. Willie slowed the truck, turned off the highway, and started down the dirt road toward Mrs. Grundy's stack lot.

He never saw the pothole in the road. I saw it and yelled, "Watch the hole, Willie!"

He slammed on his brakes and jerked the wheel to the left. He missed the hole, but when he hit the brakes about a dozen bales came crashing down on the cab. Startled, he popped the clutch, and that sent the rest of the load over the back end.

When the bales stopped falling, we looked out and saw our load of hay in the middle of Mrs. Grundy's road. Willie's face went purple.

Then I looked up and saw a little old lady walking toward us. She was wearing an apron and an old fashioned sun bonnet. She had the sweetest face you ever saw, and in the sweetest voice you ever heard, she said, "Would you boys mind putting that hay in the stack lot? It's kind of in the way out here in the road."

Willie took a deep breath and ground his teeth together. "Yas ma'am." We got out and looked at the mess. What we saw was 240 loose bales and 480 busted wires. That hay wasn't going anywhere.

Willie gave this report to Mrs. Grundy. She took it very well.

"Oh, that's all right, Willie. I understand, but I sure do hate that you went to all this trouble for nothing."

Willie blinked. "Huh?"

"I believe our arrangement was 'in the stack'. If you can't put this hay in the stack, then I suppose you'll have to take it back home."

"I can't take it back home."

Mrs. Grundy shook her head. "Mercy, that's a shame."

With that, she gave us a wink and a smile and walked back toward the house.

We climbed into the truck and roared off. "Well, Willie you really showed her," I said.

"Drop dead."

Mrs. Grundy waved good bye with a white hankie. By the time we reached the pavement, she was opening a pasture gate and turning her hungry cows in on Willie's pile of hay.

Willie's Exposure

A couple of weeks ago, Willie Onthenextranch decided he was tired of the scenery. He was tired of wind and dust and cold and snow, busting ice on tanks and feeding cows and checking windmills and doing chores.

He wanted to get off the ranch for a while and see what the world was up to.

Well, about that same time he was reading one of his cow papers and saw a story about a stockman's seminar that was going to be held in the big city. The topic for the seminar was "Ways of Exposing the Cattleman's Point of View." Right then he made up his mind that he was going to attend.

For the next several days, Willie was all business. "Our biggest problem," he said to me, "is that we can't get our story across to the journalists and consumers. Exposure, that's what we need. We've got to learn how to sell ourselves."

I just had to gig him. "Willie, I don't think that's such a big problem. For my part, the first fool that comes along and offers two cents a pound can have you. I guess if they put enough perfume in the pot, they might get a bar of soap out of you."

He gave me the evil eye. "Typical rancher. No vision or foresight. Everything's a big joke. That right there is the reason this cattle business stays in such a wreck."

To Willie, this stockman's seminar was strictly business—serious business. But just in case things got out of hand, he planned to pack a bottle of sagebrush thinner in his suitcase. I guess that's what he meant when he talked about "vision and foresight."

He sent in his money and got motel reservations. Everything was all set. He and Iris would get up early Friday morning and drive to the city, arriving there in time for the first session at two that afternoon.

The night before, he was so excited he could hardly sleep. He'd been doing a lot of thinking about the problems of the rancher, and he was looking forward to meeting some of the biggest names in the cattle industry: Jim Beam, Jack Daniels, Hiram Walker and all the others.

Friday morning at five o'clock, he flew out of bed. "Come on, Iris, get up! We got places to go, and you're burnin' daylight."

Iris, who was still cross-eyed and half asleep, looked out the window. "Burning daylight! Willie, the sun isn't even up yet."

"I don't want to be late," he growled. "Now get up and rattle your hocks."

"I don't have hocks, and if I did, I sure wouldn't rattle them at this hour of the night."

"Come on, Iris. Let's get on the road."

Half an hour later, Willie had their suitcases sitting beside the door and was ready to jump into his clothes. He was so excited he was trembling all over.

Iris entered the room. "Wait a minute. I want to see what

you're wearing." Willie squealed like a pig under a gate, but it didn't do any good.

Iris checked his outfit and shook her head in disbelief. "Willie, dear, a red tie does not go with a purple shirt, and neither one matches that brown suit, which has gravy stains on the lapels and a big hole under the left arm."

Willie howled and bellered. Iris let him howl, stood her ground, and then continued. "That suit should have gone to the dump 10 years ago. And as for your boots, dear, they would be just fine for cleaning out the chicken house, but you can't wear them to the city."

More howls. Iris went on. "Those socks don't match, and they're full of holes. You must have found them in the trash can."

"I found them in my drawer," Willie bawled. "And who's going to see my danged socks if I'm wearing boots?"

"It's the principle. Please put them in the trash and don't try to sneak them back into your drawer. Now, that T-shirt isn't fit for a dog fight. If you want to dehorn cattle in your good T-shirts, that's all right with me, but you're not going to the city looking like you'd murdered someone with an ax."

He moaned. "Iris, please! We've got to get on the road."

"We'll get on the road just as soon as you put on some decent clothes."

He cursed and raved and went to the closet. When he walked away, Iris let out a gasp. "Willie, those underpants have a hole as big as a cantelope."

He screwed himself around and looked. Sure enough, his entire left cheek was showing. But this time he wasn't going to budge. Enough was a dadgummed 'nuff. "I'll change everything else, but I'm gonna wear these shorts, hole or no hole. A man can only be pushed so far."

Iris shrugged. She had done her best. If the old goat

wanted to wear ragged drawers, just let him. "You're awfully stubborn, Willie."

"That's right," he fumed. "A man's got his pride. Now get ready."

He drove 70 and 80 all the way, and they arrived in the city at noon, with two hours to kill before the seminar started. Along the way, Willie had entertained Iris with such conversation as, "Idiot drivers! If they don't know how to drive a car, why don't they stay home."

Since they were early, Iris suggested that they have lunch at the Jolly Cowboy Steak House, a famous (and expensive restaurant). Willie said no, he wanted to take her to a quaint (and cheap) little joint that specialized in barbecue and dill pickles.

They had just sat down to plates of greasy ribs when two gunmen burst in the front door and announced that his was a holdup. After cleaning out the till, they told the patrons to sit down and shut up, and ordered all the men to strip down to their shorts.

Moments after the robbery, a newspaper photographer arrived on the scene to cover the story. In the next morning's paper, Willie's left buttock appeared on the front page.

The caption read: "Cattleman's point of view exposed at last."

As you can imagine, when Willie returned, all the cowboys in Alkali County turned out to give him a hero's welcome.

A Bad Day

Here's a little piece of advice. If you ever run into Willie Onthenextranch, don't ever start the conversation with, "Well Willie, how is everything?" Because he'll tell you.

I found that out in January. I'd finished chunking the grub at the old cows and stopped in at Willie's for sassafras tea (he quit serving coffee to company when it got expensive) and a little high level conversation about the weather.

I was feeling pretty good about things. All the cows had come in. The sun was out. The day was warm and still. The snow had started to melt off. The temperature had climbed up to 30 degrees. I'd already checked the mail box and hadn't got any duns. It looked like a fine day.

So we sat down in the kitchen over cups of Willie's swamp root tea, and I said, "Well, Willie, how is everything?"

He looked out the window for a minute and then turned back to me with kind of a fierce look. "What do you want to ask a question like that for?"

100

"Just being friendly. A guy has to say something."

"Well, everything's lousy, if you want to know."

"Really? What's the trouble?" When will I learn to keep my trap shut?

"In the first place, I'm tired of this dad-danged deep freeze son-of-a-gun Panhandle pig-nosed weather. I've been chopping ice for three weeks, and today I chopped a hole in the bottom of a tank."

"Yeah, it's been cold," I said.

"Our bathroom's been froze up for a week, and yesterday I tried to thaw out the pipes with a cuttin' torch."

"And?"

"I thawed 'em, all right—ice, pipes and all."

"Well, that's not so bad," I said. "Anybody can. . . ."

"Shut up, I ain't through. You asked how everything is, and I'm going to tell you. You ever stop to think how much money you owe the bank?"

"I'd rather not."

"Well, you ought to stop and think about it some time. I heard a guy on TV the other night who said we're in for a 50-year drouth. How are you going to pay back the banker if it don't rain for 50 years?"

"I heard the drouth was only supposed to last for 20 years," I said, trying to cheer things up.

"Yeah? Well I heard another guy say that the earth's gettin' colder. In 20 years, if we haven't dusted out, we may freeze out. And on top of that, you've got all these earthquakes in Russia and China. The Grit says that's a sign of. . . I don't remember, but it's something awful.

"Well, one nice thing about it," Willie growled, "it don't matter whether we dust out or starve out or freeze out or get earthquaked out, because we couldn't pay off our notes with cattle anyway."

"I guess there's a bright side to everything," I said.

101

"They won't be happy till they break us all. And then you take this disease business. You ever listen to the radio? Why, every 10 minutes they run some kind of warning about disease. If you ain't going blind, you're going deaf or crazy. They want us to give up cigarettes and liquor and candy bars before they kill us. Then there's always multiple cirrhosis and high blood pressure and birth defects and heart attacks. And if you don't get mowed down by one of them, that's a sign you're going to get cancer. You ever stop and think about how many things can cause cancer?"

"Willie, to be honest. . . "

"The way I get it, anything can cause cancer, and the only way to protect yourself is to quit everything. It looks like we're all as good as dead."

I stared out the window. The sun had gone behind a cloud.

"And what happens when you die?" Willie went on. "The dad-danged lawyers and politicians and undertakers move in and take whatever you didn't manage to lose on a bunch of scrawny cows. There's estate taxes and probate and funeral expenses. You've got to pay the singers and the piano player and the preacher and the gravedigger. And I'll bet they charge sales tax on coffins. Greedy ding-donged dad-danged politicians! They'd steal nickles from a crippled newsboy. They've got it rigged where a man can't afford to live, but he can't afford to die either.

"And speaking of politicians . . ." In a dramatic gesture, Willie jumped up from his chair and spit into the sink. "Speaking of drouth and plague, let's just look at our politicians. Do you know what the Intelligence Service does? Their agents work full-time trying to find signs of intelligent life in Washington, D.C. They ain't found any yet, but if they ever do, they'll throw him out of office. That's the kind of mess we're in."

102

The sky had clouded up outside, and the wind was starting to blow.

"And while we're on the subject of government, I heard the other day that one of those nincompoop federal agencies has made it against the law to wear dirty socks."

"Surely not, Willie. They wouldn't go that far."

"Ha! They've made it against the law for boys and girls to be different. They've made it against the law to pray. The Pledge of Allegiance is unconstitutional. The Star Spangled Banner discriminates against the flags of other nations. And you're telling me they don't have the gall to outlaw dirty socks? Ha!"

I sighed. I felt like I'd been run through a combine. "Willie, things are bad, but this isn't supposed to be heaven, you know."

"Heaven!" His finger came at me like a Comanche arrow. "Now there's something else. Let's just look at what heaven's going to be like. It's going to draw the dullest people in the world, and they're going to sit around singing hymns for a hundred billion years—and half of 'em can't sing to start with. Now how would you like. . . "

I couldn't stand any more. I got up and headed for the door. "I got to go, see you tomorrow, maybe."

Outside, the sun was gone, the wind was up and it was snowing. And Willie followed me all the way to the pickup.

"And in case you don't know, it's income tax time again," he said, just as I saw the flat tire on the right rear. I got the high-lift and went to work. Willie kept right on talking. "I see you don't have a new tag for your pickup. You'll have to pay a penalty." I put on the spare. "And your inspection sticker expired two months ago, and you've got a leak in your radiator."

Finally I slumped into the pickup and hit the starter. If the motor hadn't kicked off, I would have hung myself. Willie

103

leaned against the window and looked up at the sky. And, of all things, he smiled.

"You know," he said, "it's turned out to be a pretty nice day after all. It's good for a guy to talk things out once in a while."

Well, that did it. I got mad.

"Willie, that all depends on who's talking and who has to listen. If I'd had any idea the world was such a rotten place, I

never would have got out of bed this morning. I'm glad you melted your son-of-a-gun pipes, and I hope your dad-danged tanks are froze clean to China. And the only reason you don't have one of those dreaded diseases is that a germ couldn't stand your company that long."

I threw her in gear and spun off, leaving Willie standing in the snow with his mouth open.

Willie's Christmas

It was Christmas Eve. A slate gray sky was beginning to spit a few flakes of snow when I finished my feed run. I hadn't seen Willie Onthenextranch for a while, so I took the long way home and stopped in at this place.

I found him down at the barn, humped up around a little propane heater. He was sitting on a five gallon can. His chin was resting on his hand and he was glaring at a windmill head on the floor in front of him. Parts were scattered everywhere, and Willie had grease from the tip of his nose to the toes of his boots. He didn't look too happy.

"Morning, Willie," I said. He mumbled a greeting. "Let me guess. You tore into it, and now you can't get it back together."

His eyes came at me like boxing gloves. "Who asked your opinion? I'll get it back together when I'm good and ready."

"Oh. You're just not ready?"

"That's right."

"You've got to think about it for a while?"

"You're catchin' on."

"You want me to help you?"

"No, I want you to mind your own business," he snarled. "I'll get the son of a buck back together, if I have to use a sledge hammer to do it."

I shook my head. "Willie, you're just too stubborn. You'll be mad at that windmill all day. This is Christmas Eve. You're supposed to be happy. You shouldn't let a windmill head ruin your Christmas spirit."

"I won't, because I ain't got any Christmas spirit."

I gasped. "Why you old rip, that's an awful thing to say!"

"Oh yeah? Well, it's the truth. I'm fed up with Christmas. It's nothing but a big commercial rip-off. They want you to spend yourself into the poorhouse, and then they expect you to feel happy about it. In this day and age, Christmas means one thing: debts. The cattle business gives me all the Christmas I can stand. I don't need any dad-danged Santa Claus to get me in any deeper."

I tried to tell Willie that Christmas was what you made it, that it was a feeling, a state of mind. "It doesn't cost anything to sing a Christmas carol."

"Can't sing."

"Or to read the Christmas story in Luke."

"I'm a cowboy," he growled. "I get tired of reading about sheepherders and camel drivers."

"Well, it doesn't cost much to send out Christmas cards to your neighbors."

"I'd rather sue 'em than wish 'em Merry Christmas."

I sighed. "I guess there's no hope for you. You're nothing but a Scrooge."

"That's right. Close the door on your way out. I can't afford to heat the horse pasture."

"Well, all right, Willie," I said. "I hope y'all have a merry Christmas."

"Humbug."

"And I wish you lots of luck with that windmill head—all bad."

"Humbug again, humbug forever. Close that door, I'm freezing my tail."

"It's not your tail that's cold, Willie. It's your heart." With that brilliant thrust, I slammed the door and left.

Around noon, the weather got worse. The little flakes of snow that had fallen through the morning changed into big wet feathers of snow, and the wind began to blow from the north. By three o'clock the roads were getting bad. Around five Willie went outside to look at the clouds and saw a station wagon sliding down the road toward his house.

"What kind of dumb bunny would be out driving in this kind of weather?" he asked Iris, who had come to the door to look. "If they use the phone, they're gonna pay for the call."

"Willie, just hush," she said, and went out to meet the station wagon when it pulled up beside the house. Willie followed.

The lady who was driving explained that she was a Catholic sister and had taken 10 small children from an orphans home to a Christmas parade that morning. Caught in the storm, they had turned off on a county road to seek refuge.

"Wal," Willie spoke up, "the nearest motel. . . "

"Please get out, Sister," Iris cut in. "We'd be delighted to have you and the children stay with us until the storm breaks. Our kids are all grown and gone, and we'd just be tickled to have company for Christmas—wouldn't we, Willie?"

Old Willie looked at those 10 kids. Their noses were pressed against the windows, and they were staring at him with wide eyes, as though they had never seen a real live cowboy before.

"Wouldn't we, Willie?"

"Sure we would." Then, under his breath, he added,

"That's just what we've been needin' around here: 10 hungry kids, more foot rot and some smallpox."

The children got out and filed toward the house. The last child to get out was a four-year-old boy. Willie noticed that he was crying.

"What's the matter, you cold?" The lad shook his head. "Scared?" He shook his head again. "Hungry?" The boy said no. "Well, then you got nuthin' to complain about, so quit cryin'." The little fellow picked his way through the snow and continued to cry. Willie grumbled under his breath for moment, then caught the boy by the arm. "All right, son, now you tell me what's the trouble."

The boy sniffed and blinked out two more big tears. "Mister, do you think Santa Claus can find us out here?"

"Santa Claus!" Willie snorted. "On a cattle ranch? Ha! Listen, little boy, it's time you learned about this hard old world. Santa wrecked his sled and can't make it down these country roads. Sorry, but that's life."

Willie figured he had nipped that problem in the bud and there would be no more talk about Santa Claus. But as soon as the boy reached the house, he passed the word to his companions that Santa wouldn't be able to reach them, and within minutes the entire house was filled with weeping and wailing.

Out on the back porch, Willie tried to explain to his wife why he had said such a thing. "Iris, I was just trying to prepare them for life in the real world. How did I know the little snots would all start bawling?"

Iris nodded and smiled. "Willie dear, you have only one small problem. You're a sour, ill-tempered, grouchy, unbearable old snake. And if you spoil Christmas for those kids, I'm going to teach you something about the real world. You're going to eat tuna fish for the rest of your life." Willie flinched. "I'll stay up and make rag dolls for the girls, and you'd better have something for those boys."

109

"Yes, dear."

"But first, you march right in there and tell those kids that Santa Claus is coming."

"Yes dear." Willie shuffled into the living room. "Kids. . . er. . . uh. . . I just got a call on the CB radio. Santa Claus hung his sled up in a barbed wire fence and bent a runner. I'm going out to help him, and I think maybe he can make it here by morning."

The tears stopped. The children smiled and cheered. "See," Iris whispered in his ear, "it doesn't hurt to be nice once a year." Willie grumbled and marched down to the shop to make five bird houses before morning.

Two days later, I stopped in and found Willie down at the barn, fussing over that same windmill head. I asked if he'd had a nice Christmas.

"Ah, we had a bunch of danged kids here," he grumped. "They was about half nice. Kinda hated to see'em leave."

I smiled. "Willie, you're getting mellow in your old age. Next thing you know, you'll be saying that we ought to have Christmas every year."

"Wal, I don't know as I'd want to be that radical about it. Once every five years would be a-plenty. But I'll tell you one thing, Christmas beats tuna fish."

I pondered that for a moment. "You know, Willie, I think you've got something there. 'Christmas beats tuna fish.' Somehow it captures all the wonder and excitement of Christmas, the joy and. . . "

"Drop dead and hand me that wrench."

John R. Erickson is the author of 19 books and hundreds of articles. His work has appeared in the *Dallas Times Herald, Texas Highways, Western Horseman, Persimmon Hill, The Cattleman, Livestock Weekly,* and many other places. He is a member of the Texas Institute of Letters, the Philosophical Society of Texas and the Western Writers of America. He lives in Perryton, Texas, with his wife Kristine and their three children.

Drawings by Gerald L. Holmes have appeared in *Beef Magazine, Western Horseman, The Cattleman,* and other places. He has published one book of cartoons, *Pickens County,* and his work has illustrated 12 of John Erickson's books. He and his wife Carol live in Perryton with their two sons.

Printed by Cushing-Malloy, Inc., Ann Arbor, Michigan.

Designed and produced by *Innovative Publishing,* P. O. Box 580, Perryton, Texas, 79070.

MORE GREAT ENTERTAINMENT
BY JOHN R. ERICKSON

ACE REID: COWPOKE

Ace Reid: Cowpoke by John R. Erickson. Photographs and cartoons. Index. Clothbound $15.95.

This biography is a milestone in western writing, for it brings together two of the most popular humorists of our day: Ace Reid and John Erickson. When these two cowboys get together, the result is a book you won't be able to put down.

The HANK THE COWDOG Series of Books
by John R. Erickson
Drawings by Gerald L. Holmes

Hank the Cowdog

The Further Adventures of Hank the Cowdog

It's a Dog's Life

Murder in the Middle Pasture

Faded Love

Let Sleeping Dogs Lie

The Curse of the Incredible Priceless Corncob

The Case of the One-eyed Killer Stud Horse

Paperbacks $5.95 each   Hardbacks $9.95 each

JOHN R. ERICKSON'S
STORIES ON CASSETTE TAPE

Each two cassette tapeset features Erickson reading all the parts in character, plus songs, background music and sound effects.

Hank the Cowdog

The Further Adventures of Hank the Cowdog

It's a Dog's Life

Murder in the Middle Pasture

Faded Love

Let Sleeping Dogs Lie

The Curse of the Incredible Priceless Corncob

The Case of the One-eyed Killer Stud Horse

The Devil in Texas and Other Cowboy Tales

TAPESETS $13.95 each

Hank the Cowdog's Greatest Hits

Single tape $6.95

MORE GREAT BOOKS
BY JOHN R. ERICKSON

Cowboy Country. Photographs by Kris Erickson. Hardback $13.95.

The Modern Cowboy. Photographs by Kris Erickson. Paperback $6.95.

Panhandle Cowboy. Photographs by Bill Ellzey. Paperback $5.95.

The Hunter. (Historical novel) Hardback $9.95.

Essays on Writing and Publishing. (How-to book) Paperback $5.00.

COWBOY HUMOR
BY JOHN R. ERICKSON

Cowboys Are a Separate Species

Cowboys Are Partly Human

Alkali County Tales or If at First You Don't Succeed, Get a Bigger Hammer

The Devil in Texas and Other Cowboy Tales

Paperbacks $5.95 each   Hardbacks $9.95 each

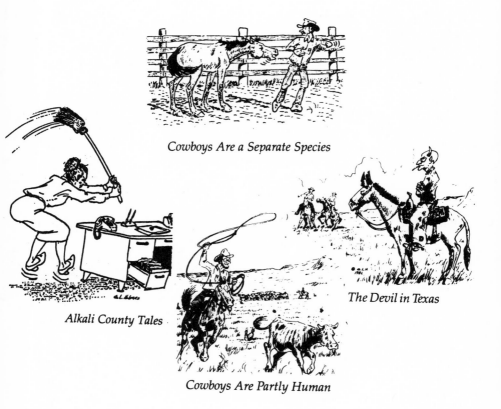

Cowboys Are a Separate Species

Alkali County Tales

The Devil in Texas

Cowboys Are Partly Human

MAVERICK BOOKS ORDER FORM

Name _____

Address _____

City _____ State _____ Zip _____

Visa/MasterCard _____ Expires _____

Visa or MasterCard orders may call 1-800-722-HANK
in Texas call 1-(806) 435-7611 . Please have your card at hand.

Description	Price	Quantity	Total

*Texas residents include **6 1/4 %**
(.0625)

Subtotal _____

**If subtotal is:

Sales Tax* _____

less than $14.00	add $1.50
$14.01 to $20.00	add $2.00
$20.01 to $30.00	add $2.75
$30.01 to $40.00	add $3.50
over $40.00	add $4.00

Postage** _____
  and handling

Total _____

Maverick Books, Inc. Box 549, Perryton, Texas 79070 / (806) 435-7611
Please feel free to reproduce this form.

MAVERICK BOOKS ORDER FORM

Name _____

Address _____

City _____ State _____ Zip _____

Visa/MasterCard _____ Expires _____

Visa or MasterCard orders may call 1-800-722-HANK
in Texas call 1-(806) 435-7611 . Please have your card at hand.

Description	Price	Quantity	Total

*Texas residents include **6 1/4 %** (.0625)

Subtotal _____

**If subtotal is:

less than $14.00	add $1.50
$14.01 to $20.00	add $2.00
$20.01 to $30.00	add $2.75
$30.01 to $40.00	add $3.50
over $40.00	add $4.00

Sales Tax* _____

Postage** _____
  and handling

Total _____

Maverick Books, Inc. Box 549, Perryton, Texas 79070 / (806) 435-7611
Please feel free to reproduce this form.